IN GOOD
COMPANY

In Good Company *is dedicated to the Big Hand Theatre Company (producing 1983–92), particularly my fellow core members Annerose de Jong, Brendan O'Connell, Jo-Anne Duncan and Manny Aston. What a blessing it is to work in the company of such talented friends!*

Special thanks and love goes to Dr Michael Shepanski, the best speller I know.

IN GOOD COMPANY

A manual for producing independent theatre

Lyn Wallis

Currency Press, Sydney

First published in 2005 by
Currency Press Pty Ltd
PO Box 2287
Strawberry Hills NSW 2012 Australia
www.currency.com.au
enquiries@currency.com.au

National Library of Australia Cataloguing-in-Publication Data:
Wallis, Lyn, 1961–.
    In good company: a manual for producing independent theatre.
    ISBN 0 86819 753 X.
    1. Theater - Production and direction - Australia. I. Title.
    792.02

Book and cover design by Kate Florance, Currency Press
Front cover shows Ben Borgia, Ben Tate and Nick Osborne in the Tamarama Rock Surfers production of Daniel Keene's *The Share*. Directed by Lee Lewis, design by Alice Babidge. Photo: Brett Boardman
Printed by Southwood Press, Marrickville

Contents

Schedules

Illustrations

Suzan-Lori Parks' *In the Blood* for B Sharp. Directed by Tanya Denny, design by Jo Lewis. Photo: Brett Boardman   *154*

Humphrey Bower and Sophia Hall in the last seen imagining production of last seen imagining's adaptation of Bernhard Schlink's novel *The Reader* for The Blue Room. Directed by Humphrey Bower and Sophia Hall. Photo: Ashley de Prazer   *170*

Thank you!

My working life is very rich, thanks to the many talented and dedicated indie artists and companies I have the privilege to hang out with. Company B must be mentioned for its incredible commitment to the 'next wave', as must my very hard-working colleagues there, and our splendid B Sharp companies.

A number of industry colleagues helped me enormously by sharing their knowledge over coffee, reading and offering feedback on chapters of the book, and generously supplying artwork and other inclusions. I am very grateful to: Katrina Berg, Wendy Blacklock, Brett Boardman (particularly for the fabulous cover shot), John Buckley, Jenni Carbins, Neil Armfield and Rachel Healy at Company B, Darlinghurst Theatre Company, Ashley de Prazer, Leith Douglas, Linden Goh, Samantha Hawker, Brenna Hobson, Tim Kliendienst, Penny Miles, Andrew Dunn and Sarah Wilson at Mollison Communications, Dr Michael Shepanski (particularly for the index), Vivian Cooper Smith, Tamarama Rock Surfers, Glenn Terry, The Blue Room, The Store Room, David Wayling, Anthony Weigh and John Woodland.

Here's a big thanks to Victoria Chance and everyone at Currency Press for supporting this project and being so encouraging!

It's important for me to acknowledge the support of my parents Peter and Judy Wallis, my sister Leanne, and also colleagues during formative years at the Q Theatre in Penrith, notably my Intensive Acting Course classmates and teachers from 1985–6, including the late Richard Brooks. This course was an extraordinary way to learn about creativity, discipline, and the power of teamwork and community spirit.

Introduction

In Good Company is a practical guide for producers of small-scale professional, co-operative and amateur theatre. It is particularly aimed at the burgeoning professional independent sector, which is currently engaged in lively and ambitious work in small to medium-sized venues right across Australia.

Not since the early days of La Mama, the Pram Factory and the Nimrod Theatre has fringe or independent theatre enjoyed such a vibrant profile as an energetic and progressive alternative to the mainstream. A new wave of high-standard independent theatre has been kick-started by the next generation of actors, directors, designers and producers eager to make their mark on the theatrical scene. Now, Sydney boasts stable independent theatre seasons hosted by Darlinghurst Theatre Company, Company B (B Sharp), the Griffin Theatre (Stablemates) and Tamarama Rock Surfers at the Old Fitzroy. In Melbourne there's the legendary La Mama Theatre, and newer ventures such as The Store Room and Red Stitch Theatre. Perth has the Blue Room and Adelaide, the long-standing Bakehouse Theatre.

The result is a new wave of artistic teams rapidly growing in ability and confidence, despite a chronic lack of resources and a dwindling number of affordable venues. They are driven by passion and talent; which of course is the fuel our industry needs for a bright and sustainable future.

An increasing number of these young theatre practitioners are willing to take on the thankless (and mostly unpaid) role as 'producer' of their colleagues' work, and yet, in my work over recent years with hundreds of small companies, I'm amazed at how inconsistent the 'independent' approach to theatre producing can be; hence I decided to write this guide.

I don't regard myself as an expert, and this is not a manual full of 'expert' advice. It's more of a rough guide. It explains how to put together a show and shape a small company from 'go to whoa'; an exercise that often reminds me of the salvage of Apollo 13 with cardboard and sticky tape. It is also shamelessly opinionated. Some experienced practitioners will not agree with everything I say, and younger ones may find better ways to do things. This is just *my* way, but it is at least a starting point for the average indie company.

I wish for readers to finish this book on a journey of research and discovery. Wherever possible, I have given pointers to websites which will help you find dedicated and genuinely 'expert' information about complex areas such as copyright, marketing and sponsorship. The symbol **[W]** followed by a number indicates a useful URL in the book's web directory which appears at the end of the book (see p. 197).

Producing is not rocket science. Good producers (be they individuals or a team of company members) have great people skills, are brilliant schedulers, pay attention to minute detail and understand the dynamics of planning and excellent timing. They know when to let the rockets off!

I have great love for independent theatre, and have written this manual for practitioners who are letting poor producing skills get in the way of their artistic output. And, although it's primarily aimed at indie theatremakers, be they dedicated producers, or simply groups of actors and directors trying to get shows up, I have tried to present the process in such a way that amateur theatre companies and theatre students. may also find it useful.

I want all your rockets to go off in a big way. If this book contributes just a little to a joyful artistic ascent, I will be a very happy writer!

Gwyneth Price, Julia Davis, Benedict Hardie and Johnny Nasser in the State of Play and B Sharp production of Joshua Lobb's *Wilde Tales*. Photo: Brett Boardman

1

In good company

Company formation, artistic drivers, team planning

A theatre company is an adventure, and adventures begin in all sorts of ways.

Let's say you are in the adventure of *independent* theatre. That proud word 'independent' calls out for freedom of motive and expression, and indeed most independent theatre projects do begin in a very free way. Here a young producer finds a hot script and draws a group of newly graduated actors together. There an experienced director decides to try some riskier work, and books a small venue. Some of the most extraordinary projects I know were hatched over a beer, or in the cramped living room of a shared apartment.

Creating a production can be a deeply satisfying experience, especially when you work alongside artistic companions who share your drive and your dream. And yet ... you might want more. An ongoing artistic venture by a recognisable team or company can bring new rewards. But how do you know when it's worth forming a company? This raises a new set of questions. If the ad-hoc arrangement was fun, why formalise the arrangement legally? Has your group got what it takes for the long haul? And, if it does, how do you transform the casual collaboration into a lasting company?

I am talking about *all* the contributors here, including (in alphabetical order) actors, designers, directors, producers, production managers and technicians. In an independent team, they have an equal right to suggest projects, and to participate in them. I call these people *collaborators*.

A group of collaborators working together in theatre is what you and I call a *company*. To lawyers, however, it isn't a company until the arrangement is formalised in certain specific ways. So, what you start with is a *company-in-name*, and later on you may (or may not) decide to form a *company-in-law*. In-laws have their good and bad points—as you probably know already, but just to be sure I will cover the subject in detail at the end of this chapter.

For now, let us consider the first stage: assembling a group of collaborators, for more than just a single show. This brings a bunch of benefits:

- The chance to develop, or participate in, works of specific personal interest.
- The satisfaction of working with like-minded individuals—people you have chosen to work with.
- An artistic 'hub', where you will find ongoing support, advice and creative opportunities.
- An opportunity (rare for artists) to develop strategic and leadership skills, and to try your hand at project management in a supportive environment.
- A 'brand' that can attract funding and resources, and help to develop an audience base.

For many collaborators, an in-name independent company is the ultimate freedom. It allows them to pursue paid work outside, and come to the company in stints, for projects they feel passionate about, without the burden of organisational duties—or so it seems. Beware! If the company is to survive then somebody, somewhere along the line, has to take responsibility for the administrative work, and serve as a phone or email contact.

Let's not worry about administrative problems yet, though. We'll come to them, as well as the in-law issues, soon enough. Right now, I assume you are keen to produce a string of vibrant, small-scale productions with your group of fabulous friends. So let's talk about what's on your mind: your desire to create brilliant, independent theatre that is meaningful, artistically satisfying, and enjoyable for your audience. In other words, the reason you got into this adventure in the first place.

The muse

Well? Why did you? The desire to create brilliant, meaningful indie theatre goes for you and every other budding company that might be reading this. You need to be more specific. You need to *identify your muse*. Only then will you understand the place of your company, and indeed the need for your company, in a world that is already brimming with theatrical hopefuls.

Your muse is the light that guides your company. It might be the light of a star: a specific person who is its artistic driver. Or there might be a constellation of stars. Some companies are very actor-driven, others respond to the very particular interests of their director. It is rarer to find companies shaped by sound, lighting, and set designers, but it happens! And such groups, with a muse-in-chief inspired by a variety of theatrical textures, can generate fascinating work.

Sometimes the muse is not a person at all but something more abstract; a mode of working, say, or a style of work, the company admires and aims to accomplish.

As a rule, I find that the most interesting and focussed groups, and the ones which last, started out as a small core of collaborators.

They might have come together because of a great idea or script, but they instinctively respond to their artistic impulses in a fundamental way, and, they later draw in people who respond to similar impulses. Without even thinking about it, these companies are finding their muse.

The muse personified

The solo act. An individual who forms their own company for the purpose of doing exactly what they like, without overt interference from anyone else. They are often seen wearing the dual hats of producer and director, generally invest their own money and gather people who are specifically suited to the project at hand. Despite repeat collaborations with one or two trusted people, essentially the 'company' belongs to them.

The leader of the pack. An individual who stands out as being more artistically focussed than anyone else. Most often this is a director or an energetic performer looking for great roles for themselves. They read or research widely and always manage to get their hands on new scripts, or generate new ideas. They respond to the needs of a larger group, but are generally recognised as the collectors or initiators of scripts and projects. The group trusts them to get the ball rolling every time. This can sometimes be a tag-team, for example, a producer and director.

The groovy group. A collection of theatreworkers keen to read, workshop and discuss. Passionately interested in devised theatre, storytelling through hybrid techniques, the re-invention of the classics or the reinterpretation of myths and legends. Can often produce a leader, but are always mindful of democratic processes.

'We are not a Muse'. To some new companies, the concept of strong, individual personalities is unimportant, or even suspect. The play's the thing, and the collaborators are there to serve it; not the other way around. If this is how you look at it, then your muse is not a person, but a mode, a type of work. Still, it's important to identify that muse as clearly as you can. Is it urging you to:

- Produce new, text-based works? If so, is it specifically new Australian scripts? Do you want to encourage new writers by running ads or competitions? Or are you looking at some edgy new international work—maybe the scripts you collected on your backpacking trips to America or the UK, which haven't been performed yet in Australia?
- Stage classic and complex texts? Perhaps you long to produce works that are rarely seen on Australian mainstages.
- Generate devised work? Can you make something like no-one else, using the varied skills of your collaborators? This includes physical, dance and design-driven theatre.
- Engage in work that is culturally specific, or politically and socially relevant?
- Create a diverse artistic environment? Do you want to defy homogeneity, by including artists of different cultural backgrounds and physical types, or who are physically or intellectually challenged?

These are only a few of an endless list of artistic drivers, and in many cases people and modes combine seamlessly to make the identity of a company. Whatever your muse, trace the basic shape of it at the start. When everyone knows what they're involved in, they can pitch their level of involvement, and support or challenge ideas to encourage the growth of the company.

Artistic direction

In mainstream companies you'll find an *artistic director* who is responsible for the creative life, profile and growth of their organisations. The role includes researching and selecting work (with the aid of literary managers and other artistic associates), programming and usually directing some of these selections. Independent companies don't always appoint an artistic director, but this work still needs to be done.

If your company is guided by a 'solo act' or a 'leader of the pack', then chances are you'll know who is setting the artistic agenda. In a 'groovy group', it's more open; any collaborator can put ideas forward, and you might meet once a week to workshop them. If your company is driven by the 'mode muse', then that mode will set a focus for your research and reading.

If you are experimenting with a one-off production, pay good attention to:

● The match of artists and material—choose a work that fits the profile and abilities of your team or, conversely, select people who suit the demands of the work.

● The effect the work might have on the team—will it promote the team's artistic development, or its public image? What is the artistic flavour and weight of the work?

● The readiness of the text for performance—can you really address all the dramaturgical needs of a new Australian script in a one-off context (and four weeks of part-time rehearsal)?

If you are programming more than one production in a year then you should return to 'the Muse' above, and identify what drives the collaboration. If the group doesn't have a particularly strong muse, in the form of either person or mode, then plan in a way that won't lock you into an artistic straightjacket. You needn't make a decision to do only new Australian work, or only international or devised work. Play with a range of material; it may help you to find your muse as your go.

You should be aware, though, that audience and industry figures are watching you. Every piece you produce contributes to your profile and conveys something about your general artistic direction. The golden rule, if you are serious about the company, is to read widely and always choose quality material. As obvious as this sounds, many companies neglect to research all the great work that is out there, and instead choose the first thing that has a bit of sex appeal (and maybe a part for everyone).

The company can target quality scripts by:

- Researching new Australian works through peak bodies like Playworks **[W1]**, the Australian Script Centre **[W2],** and the Australian National Playwrights' Centre **[W3]**. Check out organisations that collect and read new works such as Parnassus' Den **[W4]** or that run playwriting competitions or new writing initiatives such as Naked Theatre Company **[W5]**.
- Scanning websites of international theatre companies, drama publishers such as Currency, Faber and Faber, and Nick Hern Books, and press for new works; or visiting performing arts bookshops (which often let you browse lengthily before you buy).
- Seeing lots of productions and chasing up other works by writers you admire. If you travel, make an effort to see works by independent companies, who often get their hands on great new scripts rejected by the mainstream.
- Dipping into the canon of past Australian works or acquainting yourself with less frequently produced classics.
- Talking to the Literary Managers of theatre companies.

Can I be Hamlet?

That's a scary question and the best answer might be, 'Well, you can audition'. Just because someone is a core member of the group, doesn't mean they have the right to, well, play Hamlet. You can of course run things that way, but you have to be prepared to pay the price if the actor isn't up to it. The same goes for just about any role in the company, including producing.

When a company comes together around a script for one production, then the script might come with an actor or actors attached (because they found it), and in that context it's probably fine. In any more permanent collaboration, however, it's best that a script come to the table unattached. One might reasonably expect that a director would want to work on something they have unearthed and are passionate about (and if it's a solo act muse in operation, there won't be a choice!); but if the group genuinely feels that the match isn't good, then concerned collaborators should speak up. This is where the notion of 'serving the work' comes in. Do you all want to serve the play and create the best production you possibly can? Yes? Then audition for Hamlet.

The game of the name

You'll be amazed at how quickly a good name can put a group on the map. A name that is gathering positive profile can open doors and switch on light bulbs in people's heads. Imagine your company name's as a rubber stamp that gets pounded on flyers, ads, reviews and press stories again and again—with very little effort you've already made your first steps toward company branding.

If your team plans to mount more than one production, then you should workshop a business name and register it with the appropriate state or territory body. In NSW for example, the registering body is the Office of Fair Trading (OOFT) **[W6]**; a full list of state bodies is available on the Australian Government's Business Entry Point site **[W7]**. You can do a national name check online with the Australian Securities and Investments Commission (ASIC) **[W8]**. You should do the check even if you are not intending to formally register the name. It would be more than inconvenient to discover that you cannot use the name you are advertising as you prepare for opening night!

You don't have to be a company-in-law to register a business name, and simply registering it does not create a legal entity. It does however allow you to open a bank account in the business name, for the purposes of handling production income and expenditure.

The name of a company, as with children, is often for life, so it's important that you choose one that can weather a few changes in artistic climate. As much as 'Strolling Ham Players' might be fun for a quickie fringe festival show, it could feel like an ill-fitting boot five years later, when you're pitching a ground-breaking work to the Melbourne International Festival. You may think that will never happen, but in the early stages of growth it doesn't hurt to eye off slightly bigger shoes than you need right now.

When workshopping your company name:

- Consider a title that expresses the quality, energy and interests of the group, rather than one that locks you into a particular form or genre, unless that's how you want to be defined and branded ('Bell Shakespeare' is an obvious example of this). While 'Strolling Ham Players' sounds whimsical, 'Stuck Pigs Squealing' suggests an altogether more serious animal. It says 'edgy', 'uncomfortable and unsettling', 'a bit too loud' and 'can't be ignored', which is perfect for the innovative Melbourne independent company that devised this title for itself.

- Reconsider the need to tag 'Theatre Company' or 'Productions' on the end. You have at most about five words to play with, so why not make them work for you, without wasting two to state the obvious? Some great tagless titles include 'Crying in Public Places', 'Hair of the Dog', 'Gravity Feed', 'Legs on the Wall', 'Strange Fruit', 'eRTH', 'Kicking and Screaming', 'The Men Who Knew Too Much', 'Search Party' and, my favourite from an independent company in Perth, 'last seen imagining'. Tagless titles also give you room to move, should your company wish to branch into film, television or design work.

- Make time to play with words. Set up a meeting and a whiteboard, and get each collaborator to come armed with favourite words and phrases, famous quotes, poems, rhymes, song lyrics, bits of speeches, and a bottle of something inspiring. Fill the whiteboard with words that express how you aim to affect an audience, and how you want the industry and the public to perceive you. Play word association games. Ask friends (particularly those not involved in theatre). Run a competition through your email networks. Finally, choose three names and test them out on family, taxi drivers and local shopkeepers. Only when you are fully satisfied that a set of words expresses the essence of the group, is flexible enough to allow growth and, importantly, appeals to external ears, should you settle on a name.

The producers

In the world of fully-paid professional theatre, an artistic director would have for each production a full complement of designers, a production manager, a rehearsal room, a season stage manager (and maybe ASM), a costume co-ordinator and so forth. The employing company would very likely have an in-house marketing and publicity department and graphic designer, and would act as overall producer of the work, under the watchful eye of a general manager or administrator.

The independent situation is rarely so richly resourced! And yet individuals in a co-op who eagerly take on creative and production roles, may be less keen on sharing producing tasks. The reality is that, in the absence of a nominated 'producer', producing responsibilities need to be delegated among the company.

The designated producer

The obvious best-case scenario for an indie company is to have a dedicated producer or producing team to work on an ongoing basis. This person or team should think about and plan for long term issues, such as funding strategies and touring opportunities, and monitor the progress of the company.

The second best solution is to have an individual producer attached to *each show* the team produces—not necessarily the same person each time. The producer shouldn't have to execute every task personally, but would ideally:

● Oversee the overall facilitation of the show.
● Act as the key point of contact for all 'departments' and ensure that everyone is communicating.
● Take responsibility for budgets and financial management as well as copyright and insurance issues.
● Ensure the proper execution of the marketing and publicity campaign.
● Promote and track ticket sales in advance of and during the run.
● Reconcile monies with the venue and make sure all service providers and collaborators are paid, and that relevant reports are circulated to the team.

In a production context, the producer is one part of a core facilitation team, along with:

● An artistic representative (usually the director), to whom any creative issues can be referred and who has final say in this area.
● A production or stage manager, who liaises with designers and set builders and schedules bump-in/out. This person may run the production budget, but reports to the producer.

Core collaborators and producing

If you decide not to have a single producer, divide the *producer's role* among the core collaborators. Leadership is essential, and key producing tasks are more likely to be dealt with efficiently if done by people with an ongoing investment in the company. These responsibilities include:

- Budgeting and financial management.
- Investigating legal issues, rights, insurances and signing of contracts.
- Managing the marketing and publicity campaign.
- Scheduling (rehearsal, technical).
- Troubleshooting and conflict resolution.
- Leading the fundraising drive.

Naturally the duties should be assigned according to experience and interest. Someone with great attention to detail and accuracy might be excellent for managing finances, but lack the people skills and relentless determination needed to hunt down arts editors for stories. Try to delegate fairly; it's unrealistic to expect one person to be the accountant *and* the publicist. Don't underestimate the value of a good troubleshooter. Treat this as an important role and delegate it to someone in the company who is patient, fair, stays calm in a crisis and has the respect of the majority of the collaborators. When conflicts arise, your trouble-shooter can liaise with the relevant parties. You could also consider giving them final say on minor issues, so that small conflicts are resolved quickly without disrupting the production too much. This would automatically be part of a designated producer's job.

Ring-ins and producing

There are times when a company will invite external parties into the group (who may later become core collaborators). These people will include actors, designers and directors. In my view it is important that everyone who takes part in an independent theatre collaboration should take on some producing-related duties, such as:

- Helping to identify fundraising targets;
- Set-building, prop and costume sourcing and bumping in/out;
- Poster and flyer distribution; or
- Individual marketing through personal contacts.

Sharing the load maintains company goodwill. Chances are no-one is getting paid and it's not fair to join an independent production and expect to do nothing but the fun stuff. If a collaborator is completely hopeless at everything but acting, ask them to do a weekly leafleting run through the cafes, libraries and laundromats in their local area.

Company navigation

Many of the small companies I have dealt with don't see any value in formulating or recording their goals. 'What's the point', they ask, 'when the company only exists to mount one to three productions a year?'

The fact is that goal-setting is useful and satisfying, even if your production output is quite small. For one thing, it helps you to notice how many aims you actually have. Productions are the visible tip of the iceberg; there are bound to be more, such as developing an audience base, or setting an agenda for gathering new and inspiring material. Also, by breaking your goals down into simple strategies and outcomes and attaching a timeframe, you can ensure that things actually get done. If you have a dedicated producer within your ranks, they can help lead the company through this process, so that decisions are documented and distributed amongst collaborators.

Write down as much or as little as you want. It is an investment in the venture. If you're going to bother setting up a company, no matter how small, why not get the most out of it? It's not as much work as you might think.

Your navigation chart is an informal document; a more flexible version of the rigorous 'multi-year business plans' that arts funding bodies will require later, if you seek ongoing funding. The boards and management committees of funded companies engage in strategic planning sessions, complete with SWOT (Strengths, Weaknesses, Opportunities, Threats) sessions and the thrashing out, remodelling or refining of Mission and Vision statements. All things going well, your company will be ready for serious business planning at some point in the future, but for now all you need is a simple plan for moving forward.

The Navigation Chart

The Company Navigation chart I describe here is a very basic planning document. It has only four components: a Company Character Statement, Major Goals, Strategies, and Outcomes. This document can be as brief as one page, and could include all your goals for a year. If you are nervous about planning that far ahead without resources, then do one for six months or at the very least three. As your company grows in confidence and reputation, your navigation document should become more sophisticated; a little longer in its range and a truer reflection of the company's individuality. For now, start with something simple that gets things moving, without locking you into a shape that can't grow with you. Remember, this is not a document that you need to show to anyone else, so you can be as creative with it as you like!

Schedule 1 shows a Navigation Chart for the fictional company, 'The Flying Pigs'. TFP is a physical theatre company, interested in creating shows that discuss social and political issues in Australia. Their shows are based on daring body-work, using live musicians and some words. They are happy to be labelled as a bit confrontational and keep their skills honed through constant training.

Company Navigation Chart—components

Company Character Statement: treat this as a precursor to a more formal Mission Statement: what the company does and what defines it. Once a Mission Statement is set, it should last a long time, but you can refine your Character Statement as often as you reset your Navigation Chart (every three, six or twelve months).

The Character Statement should reflect who you are, what you do, who you do it for and why. Try and use words that communicate the values and uniqueness of your company. The statement should be definitive and in the present tense ('Vodka Varmints produces fantastic contemporary Russian plays', rather than 'Vodka Varmints wants to …'). Remember that you are part of a creative enterprise, so feel free to use words that reflect the artistic spirit of your venture. Try to avoid overused 'buzz' words, such as 'excite', 'innovative', 'challenge', 'excellent'. In the Character Statement for TFP, I have replaced these with 'thrilling', 'feeds the curiosity of' and 'surprising'. Grab a thesaurus and your imagination and play! Keep asking yourselves 'Who, What and Why?'. Keep the statement to one or two sentences.

Major Goals: the broad issues you want to address. These are the big, thick branches on the planning tree. You don't need any more than four to eight of these, when you're starting out. Choose large goals that you can break down into smaller activities.

Strategies: these words express how you want to achieve your goals in a very practical way. They are the smaller activities that make up the major goals.

Outcomes: imagine you are at the end of your first navigation period, asking yourself what you've achieved. The outcomes are the desirable answers, the measurable things that indicate accomplishments.

SCHEDULE 1: Flying Pigs Navigation Chart 1: January–December

CHARACTER STATEMENT: The Flying Pigs present thrilling company-devised theatrical works, which respond to contemporary Australian issues through the use of dynamic physicality, music and words. Our training and production processes feed the curiosity, interests and abilities of our company members, and present surprising productions that question our audience's perception of their homeland.

GOALS	STRATEGIES	OUTCOMES
1. To provide ongoing development oportunities to company members	1.1 Provide regular meeting points 1.2 Encourage members to seek other training opportunities	• Instituted a two-hour training session each week • Employed four guest tutors for one session each throughout the year • Used a proportion of membership fees to provide skills development training through courses
2. To generate original material for workshops, creative development and productions on an ongoing basis	2.1 Research current issues of interest 2.2 Research audience attitudes	• Membership gathered once per month to table material and ideas • Instituted a library of cuttings and AV material for use of members • One member assigned to vox pop in shopping centres once per month • Questionnaire on current affairs distributed at performances
3. Create and perform meaningful and challenging shows that respond to the Australian environment	3.1 Research, plan, cast and crew original works 3.2 Maximise asset of previous show	• One creative development period for new show completed • One new production mounted at local venue • Remount one previous show at interstate fringe festival

GOALS	STRATEGIES	OUTCOMES
4. To interact with preferred venues, festivals and seasons	4.1 Ensure up-to-date information on costings and application dates	● Venue and fringe season info researched, updated and maintained
	4.2 Keep venues etc abreast of our activities	● Directors/venues invited to every show
		● Met with one new venue/director every two months
5. To develop our audiences	5.1 Capture data about our audiences	● Questionnaires seat-dropped at performances
		● System for legally capturing emails instituted
	5.2 Keep audiences up-to-date with our activities	● Monthly e-letter developed
		● Incentives package for regular attendees developed
6. To develop our financial base	6.1 Increase funding for productions	● Funding and philanthropic avenues researched
		● Applied to State funding body for 1 production
		● 1 in-kind and one ($5,000) cash sponsor secured for each production
	6.2 Nurture and service existing sponsors	● Disseminate monthly e-letter to sponsors
		● Develop special deals for sponsors
7. To maintain high standards of compliance and work practice	7.1 Ensure up-to-date knowledge of OH&S practice and insurance issues	● Create a procedures manual
		● Annual review of procedures
		● 1 company member to attend OH&S course

Incorporation (vs. incarceration)

Let's get back to some of the legal issues surrounding company formation.

The most common business structures are sole traders, partnerships, companies and trusts. In the eyes of the law, a company-in-name is nothing more than a group of individuals; one or more sole traders or an informal partnership. Contracts, hire agreements and leases then have to be signed by one or more individuals, who must take on all the legal responsibilities themselves.

The grave disadvantage is that if one member of the group acts negligently, or criminally, or causes injury to someone, then another member (or members) are legally liable. Many ad-hoc ventures operate in dangerous ignorance of the law, but the risk of being sued is very real.

Consider this: most independent companies operate on the smell of an oily rag, in venues that might not strictly meet compliance. Add to that the pressure and lightning speed of under-resourced bump-ins and the unaffordability of professional tradesmen. Accidents happen. There have been horror stories that involve serious loss of property (and family property!).

At the very least, the producer should draw up a simple agreement for everyone involved to sign, which outlines the intent of the collaboration. MEAA [W9] has produced a standard co-operative agreement which its members can access and which you can modify according to your needs. Public Liability insurance is also a must; in fact it is now almost impossible to hire rehearsal space or a venue in Australia without adequate Public Liability insurance.

Forming a company or association

Deciding on a formal structure is a serious undertaking, and potentially a complex one. It's wise to consult an accountant or solicitor to discuss the full range of options available, unless you are considering a standard not-for-profit option.

If you are developing a highly commercial enterprise that would never be eligible for, nor require government or philanthropic funding ('Flintstones on Ice!'), then you might consider forming a 'for profit' company. Most theatre companies have a not-for-profit status, which makes them eligible to apply for government assistance through state and federal arts funding bodies.

Most not-for-profit enterprises provide a service to, or enhance the life of the community in some way; they are not established to make a profit for investors. Not-for-profit does not mean your productions cannot make money; it's just that the money cannot be distributed as dividends to the members. Members of a not-for-profit organisation can still be employed (or be remunerated as part of an income-sharing arrangement) for specific services such as acting, designing and directing but if the organisation winds up remaining funds cannot be claimed by members.

The two most common types of not-for-profit business structures for theatre companies are Companies Limited by Guarantee (public companies) and Incorporated Associations.

A Company Limited by Guarantee does not have shares, and the liability of the members is limited to a nominal amount detailed in the company's constitution (usually a few dollars). It costs a lot to set up a company and there are more onerous reporting duties than for Incorporated Associations, but Companies Limited by Guarantee are registered with ASIC and can trade nationally. This structure is often used by companies who receive large amounts of funding and who have a significant trading relationship with the public.

Incorporated Associations are registered in the state or territory in which the enterprise is based. This structure offers a reasonable range of benefits to small groups, is not expensive to set up and has moderate reporting duties.

I must stress that a group must decide for themselves which structure best suits their chosen range of activities. Do some research. Start with the Federal Business Entry Point site **[W7]**, which provides links to excellent state sites.

Nevertheless, let's take the Incorporated Association as the typical structure for a small team—the sort of team that mounts two to four independent productions a year in venues of 50 to 150 seats. The benefits of forming an Incorporated Association are that it:

- Allows the team to act as a legal body rather than as a group of individuals. It can sign contracts, hire agreements and leases.
- Limits the legal liability of individuals to a reasonable extent.
- Allows the team to apply directly for government funding.
- Ensures the team's continuity even if collaborators withdraw.
- Gives you credibility with potential financial partners (sponsors, investors) and a secure way for them to contribute.
- Allows you to accept gifts and bequests.
- Allows the buying and selling of property.

Briefly, you are required to adopt a set of Rules (constitution), appoint a Committee (Management Committee or Board) and a Public Officer (Secretary). The company must also hold an Annual General meeting (AGM) within every calendar year.

The Committee exists to manage the affairs of the Association. It must:

- Keep up-to-date records and contacts of all members and office bearers.
- Take minutes of meetings.
- Maintain proper financial records.
- Have a common seal (an official stamp with company details on

it) which can be used by the Public Officer with the approval of the Committee.

Committee members cannot be remunerated for their activities as committee members, but they can be paid for their other activities, as can actors, designers or anyone else who provides a service to the Association.

The Public Officer is the primary contact. He or she lodges documents for the company, and ensures that the Committee meets its primary management and reporting responsibilities. The Association can also have a general membership and can charge a membership fee. New (ordinary) members can be nominated by existing members and their applications are accepted or rejected by the Committee. All paid-up members of the Association are entitled to vote at the AGM and can be nominated for office at AGMs.

At the AGM, the Committee provides the membership with documents that show the financial position of the organisation (Income and Expenditure statements and a balance sheet if there are assets). Reports on the year's artistic activities can also be presented and, finally, office bearers for the coming year are elected.

To Inc or not to Inc?

No-one other than the collaborators can decide whether or not to turn a company-in-name into a company-in-law. Independent companies that are artistically driven by less than five people often continue to operate casually, as they feel it protects their artistic control. Despite the truth in this, the downside is that it doesn't allow for change and growth. If three key people drop the ball to pursue other interests, a lot of good work can go to waste. An Incorporated Association can continue to thrive through changes in membership.

At the start of an Incorporated Association's life, its committee is usually made up of the most passionate artistic collaborators; the ones with the ideas and energy to get things started. Those people will usually 'appoint' themselves as Artistic Directors or Co-ordinators or Administrators, to ensure some artistic control over what has essentially been their baby.

In time, however, and with a growing membership, artistic direction can change. At an AGM all members have the right to voice opinions on issues put forward, to vote and to be nominated for office by other members. Whilst it might seem unlikely, you should bear in mind that strong opposition to artistic direction or internal conflict could lead to a disgruntled faction voting their own representative onto the committee, in effect staging a coup. If you limit membership to avoid this, you lose the benefits a supportive membership can bring, including positive growth and longevity.

Fear of conflict and change shouldn't get in the way of the company enjoying all the benefits incorporation can bring. If you choose not to incorporate you are legally vulnerable as individuals when it comes to insurance issues and the actions of your collaborators. It is also harder for you to access government funding, or to attract investors and partners. If you decide against it, you can still register a business name and you can apply for government grants through an auspicing party.

If you already have a good relationship with an incorporated organisation (such as a venue or an established theatre company), or if you know of one that is particularly aligned with your objectives, you could ask them to auspice a grant on your behalf. The auspicing organisation receives any grant monies and releases them to your company, monitoring how they are spent, and ensuring that reporting duties are carried out. They may charge an auspicing fee, between 5 and 20%, depending on the size and nature of the grant, and you can include that fee in your budget. For a first grant, auspicing can be a really good option as it can offer a source of professional advice and support. The level of mentorship is best negotiated with an organisation that already supports your work, and it can be used as a plus point in your application!

To Inc or not to Inc? It's entirely up to you! You can see I lean towards the 'yes' side, but I strongly advise that you toss all the issues around before making a decision. For a small company that has initially gathered individuals around a great project, it makes sense to get through one or possibly two productions before creating a legal structure. But do sign a Letter of Agreement and get basic insurances sorted out before you hit the rehearsal room. If you're still enthusiastic after two productions and feel those ideas bubbling away, then start thinking about firming things up. Good company can be hard to find, so if you have the magic, go for it!

2

Hunting and gathering

Venues and seasons, playscript and music copyright, insurances

You've found a play that you love, you have a great team assembled and you're ready to build the creative engine of your project. You just need a workshop and a launching pad.

The reality is, finding the right platform to create and finally propel your production into existence can be even harder than building the rocket. Depending on where you live, you may find a chronic shortage of rehearsal spaces and a dearth of affordable venues. Each capital city has its own strengths and challenges in this area. Sydney has a number of venues devoted exclusively to independent work in curated seasons (such as Darlinghurst Theatre Company, Tamarama Rock Surfers at the Old Fitzroy Hotel, and B Sharp at Downstairs Belvoir St Theatre), which have together created thriving hotbeds of small-scale theatre activity that are the envy of other cities. Outside of these seasons, however, there is only a handful of decent venues. Griffin Theatre Company now offers the Stables for its curated 'Stablemates' season of indie work and there are halls for hire such as the Bondi Pavillion and Newtown Theatre. Others suffer from minimal technical facilities and support, low seating capacities, lack of booking services, low profile with audiences or the tyranny of distance from the city centre. Yet even the most technically inadequate venues are often booked up to a year in advance.

Melbourne, on the other hand, has numerous affordable venues that seem to spring up out of nowhere during its lively festival periods, partly due to less rigid licensing laws. The extraordinary range and atmosphere of these places has helped to mark Melbourne as a prime generator of distinctive and risk-taking independent fare. Yet despite the amazing output of historic La Mama's unique venues and the rising profile of The Store Room in the north of the city, the Melbourne scene has for some time lacked the support of a curated season driven by the mainstream. This is now being addressed by Malthouse Theatre with its new Tower Theatre initiative. On the other side of the country, Perth's fringe theatre life is underscored by the nurturing hubs of the Blue Room and Perth Institute of Contemporary Arts (PICA), but growth there is also hampered by a minimal number of venues available for hire and the fact that many of them (like the formerly grand Rechabites Hall) are in a state of disrepair.

Aside from lobbying local councils and state and federal governments for help in establishing more and better resourced venues, the only choice most independent companies have is to rely on two powerful tools that are always at their disposal: research and planning.

The rehearsal room

Your company may be fortunate enough to have its own rehearsal space or you may be lucky enough to nab one of the few regular affordable spaces in your area. There is huge instability in room availability in capital cities and it's not even worth listing any here because chances are most of them won't be operating in a year's time! If you are producing three or more shows a year it's worth investing time, money and effort in trying to procure a rehearsal venue that you can work in on a regular basis. If your company's regime includes training and workshops, core collaborators could consider the lease of a small studio, with the option of hiring it out to trusted outsiders during fallow periods.

Whatever your circumstances, get all core collaborators to do some lateral thinking and research the less traditional options. There are many public and private premises that have significant downtime in their normal usage, though you may find it more difficult if you are planning to rehearse during the evenings and weekends. Start with who you know. Does someone in the group have connections with primary and high schools (revisit your alma mater!), scout halls, churches, libraries, after-school dance studios, day-care centres and council premises (even the smaller town halls have carpeted function rooms)? Have you noticed a warehouse or office space that has remained unleased for a lengthy period? Do a walking tour of your local area and get friendly with local real estate agents. Does one of your cash sponsors have access to lunch, board or function rooms that could be accessed on weekends or evenings? Try to negotiate lower hire or rental fees by offering some service such as helping out on a local fundraiser, running a one-off workshop for staff or giving a small percentage of a show's takings to a favourite charity. You'll find many of these non-traditional options easier if the company can find a personal connection and has insurances in place.

It's important that you find a room in which you can work comfortably. If you are going for a less traditional option, you will probably have to make significant compromises; if you're doing a two-hander with a chair and a table, working around the obstacles won't be much of a problem. If the company is mounting a larger production and has a reasonable budget for rehearsal space, then devise a checklist before checking out the options and always consider:

- Size and accessibility—there should be at *least* enough room to fit the entire stage area and for the director and stage manager to move around/sit comfortably in front of the stage area. Do you have reasonable access to the venue (decent blocks of uninterrupted time)? How many other groups use it during the week? Can you store props there safely? Is there a lockable area for valuables?

- If you are using elevation (levels or a rake) in your production, it's always best to find a room that can accommodate a rehearsal version of this. Check the width of doors and stairs for the bump-in and out of large set items.

- Light and temperature—is there good natural light during the day? Fluorescent lighting can be very draining; if that's all there is, is it possible to set-up lamps to create softer lighting for night-time rehearsals? Is the room warm enough for working in winter and cool enough for the summer? Is there adequate airflow (and windows that open)?

- External noise and room resonance—will you have to battle lots of street noise (can you open the windows in summer and still hear yourselves speak)? Are there other people in the building who won't tolerate rehearsal noise? Are the sound dynamics of the room adequate? If it's a text-based piece too much resonance could prove infuriating, whilst shows with music may want a little more 'bounce' in the sound dynamic.

- Flooring—do you need a sprung floor for movement? Is a fully carpeted floor going to interfere with the moving of props or manual sound effects? Is a wooden floor going to wreak havoc on knees and shins? Each production will have entirely different requirements. Remember that the floor of a room is the canvas upon which you are creating your work, so make sure it is at least level and clean with no splinters or impediments to free and easy movement.

- Amenities—is there easy access to clean toilets and a kitchenette? Are there enough power points in the room for any external lighting sources, sound equipment and fans or heaters you may need? Is there free parking in the area? Is it close to public transport and reasonably safe to get to and from if you are rehearsing into the late evening? Is the location convenient for the majority of the team?

Performance venues

One of the most significant trends affecting indie artists in recent years has been the establishment and cultivation of curated seasons by well-established venues. I will refer to these as *Season hubs*, as they not only provide subsidised theatre spaces for talented companies, but often act as gathering places, allowing traditionally isolated indie artists to engage with each other and access the advice of experienced theatre practitioners. Landing a berth in a season hub means you will receive more support than in 'hall-for-hire' venues. You will be entitled to a free or heavily subsidised venue and generic marketing support. On the other hand, competition for season hub slots can be fierce and you may also be restricted in the way you can present or promote your project. How does it affect the company if you can't work with your chosen publicist or you don't have the final say on your brochure image? Any season partners you choose to bring on board will have a stake in your production and a right to make suggestions and requests. Think carefully about what you are trying to achieve with a particular show and the development of your company's profile before assuming that the benefits of a curated season will outweigh those of working more independently.

Joining the season hub-bub

Every curated season has its own programming style and offers different levels of support. The core of most 'deals' is the waiving of theatre hire fees, in return for a percentage of the show's box office income (venues may take up to 30%). Some curated season deals also include a technical operator and significant levels of marketing and publicity support. Take some time at the start of the year to gather closing dates and submission criteria for each one, as well as theatre dimensions, audience capacity and technical specifications. Check interstate options if you think the piece might be suitable for touring.

Some companies choose a piece and apply to every season hub, but this is not necessarily the best way of ensuring the right home for your work. No amount of producer or venue support will make up for huge artistic compromises. The success rate for applications to curated seasons is also quite low. The three major independent seasons in Sydney, for example, program less than 8% of work submitted. So how do you raise your chances of joining the season hub-bub?

Almost all seasons ask for core production information, which generally includes a project description, budget and marketing plan, and details of personnel. It's basically a 'who, what, how and why' exercise. I have assessed many hundreds of applications in recent years and nearly all unsuccessful applications have failed to answer these questions with sufficient clarity. Lack of detail and poor choice of material puts many promising companies out of the running. To increase your chances of being programmed:

● Read the criteria thoroughly and highlight or underline the major points. These *must* be addressed clearly and succinctly. Seriously, don't leave anything out! Try reading between the lines too. What sort of picture forms in your head when you put it all together? If there are lots of words and phrases like 'cutting edge', 'risk-taking', 'experimental', then be honest with yourself about whether your work fits into this category or not. An ill-judged application not only wastes your time, but it creates a bad impression since it conveys to the curator that you don't understand or care about what is being asked of you.

- See lots of work at the venue you are applying to so that you get a genuine feel for the sort of work they are interested in.

- Research madly and avidly. Pursue great scripts or materials that will help you create great shows. This may mean browsing international websites, chasing up potentially interesting plays and paying an advance against royalties to secure hot material to avoid it being snaffled by another company. Look for scripts that meet the standards and skills of your actors. A great acting company doesn't compensate for poor writing or lacklustre ideas.

- Flesh out the list of personnel as much as you can. Curators understand that it's not always possible in a co-op situation to guarantee every single person you want for your project, but they will want a good proportion of your list confirmed. This is becoming more critical as competition for spaces and venue investment increases. Expectations in this regard will vary with the size of the project. If you require a cast of ten performers of specific ethnicity, you may not need to have the whole team on board at the time of applying, but you will need to prove to the curator that you have credible casting strategies in place. An application for a two-hander with only one actor identified or a solo show without an actor confirmed are sure to go to the bottom of the pile. As production standards in this sector increase, it's also becoming really important for venues to know and trust the design team.

- Identify your producer or producing team and emphasise their skills. The two aspects of your proposal scrutinised by any type of curated season are your *artistic* and *producing* strengths. Give them equal weight in your application. A curator may pass on an artistically interesting project if they believe the team is disorganised or won't have sufficient producer leadership, particularly during their pre-production period.

- Most venues will ask for a project description with a word or page limit, which means they want you to talk *succinctly* about what you are doing and why you are doing it. Avoid long disquisitions about your artistic theories and interests and use the words to paint a vivid and lively picture of what you are specifically trying to achieve with this project. Be as expressive as you like, steer clear of bureaucratic language and try as hard as you can to plant a juicy image of your show in the reader's head.

- Explain the extraordinary. If you team is mostly based overseas, then talk about how they are going to get (and survive) here. If expenditure in your budget is huge, let the reader know how you intend to raise the money and if there is any financial fallback position.

- Curated seasons are always keen to support new Australian work, but they are just as interested in the *quality* of it. If you submit an early draft script, indicate how the company intends to approach the development of the work (dramaturgy/workshopping). If you don't feel confident in the script or the writer, then don't submit it.

- Your first task is to get shortlisted. The more information that is missing from your written proposal (gaps in personnel, budget) the less likely this is. Curators don't have time and won't chase missing details, so make sure you flesh the project out as much as you possibly can.

- Ensure your proposal is truthful (don't fib about performance rights or personnel) and avoid personal criticisms of other artists or seasons.

- Fancy packaging is eye-catching, but won't get you any closer to the shortlist. Effort is better spent checking spelling and grammar and making sure your budget figures add up.

● When you've put it all together, show it to someone who isn't involved in the project and get them to explain what they see when they read it. Ask yourself, what is missing from this picture?

If your project is rejected, learn not to take it personally. Remember programming is highly subjective and it does not mean your proposal was not well-regarded. A curator may really enjoy your work, yet feel it isn't right for their venue. Sometimes companies miss out due to circumstances beyond their control. For example, your script (or scripts by the same writer) may turn up in other submissions or several projects may have similar themes. Curators like diversity, and won't want to program three plays about 'topic x' in the same year. If there is a feedback mechanism in place, use it. It's easy to build up reasons for rejection in your imagination and you may find that your fears are completely unfounded. Don't stop inviting the curator to see your work, as they may be able to help you with another opportunity (such as personally recommending your work to another season). *Never* abuse the person who has assessed it; you want to be remembered for talent and tenacity, not for tantrums or tartness. There is one final factor that really is beyond your control. Whilst every applicant knows how good their proposal is, only the curator knows how fantastic they *all* are!

The best way to develop relationships with curators (and venues generally) is to maintain regular and unobtrusive contact. Invite them to your shows and generally keep them up to date with what you are doing. Season curators receive several invitations to shows a day, and it isn't possible for them to attend them all. This doesn't mean they aren't tracking what groups are up to! A friendly email every few months letting them know what is coming up for you is a good way to stay on the radar. The surest way to be noticed, however, is to produce great shows that producers will trip over themselves to see! Curators will not often take risks on a first-time company (or even on a company's first application to their season), but will be very interested in teams that produce consistently strong work in a range of venues.

Halls for hire

There are venues in all states that offer performance slots in their theatres without setting too many artistic restrictions. As competition for affordable spaces increases, though, many halls-for-hire (HFH) are becoming choosier about projects, and you may find they have a selection process even for this. If the venue has a good profile and is also home to a curated season for part of the year, then it can be almost as hard to obtain a hire slot as a season berth.

The big difference for the independent producer of course, is that you are paying good money and you should make sure you get value for it. Some spaces are considerably cheaper than others, but usually offer minimal access to services and equipment. Make sure that the savings you make on a cheaper venue don't add up to a false economy. When checking out HFH, consider the following:

- Theatre configuration, size of venue and seats—will the shape of the space (proscenium arch, semi or fully in the round, open plan etc) serve the artistic needs of the play? Consider the length of the play and the comfort of your audience—will they be able to handle three hours of Shakespearean tragedy on plastic chairs at floor level? Are there air-conditioning and heating facilities?
- Performance times—are there restrictions on when and how many times you can perform each week?
- Booking facilities—not all small venues offer a booking service. If not, someone trustworthy in the company (and not living in a share house!) will have to use their phone number and an answering machine to take bookings. Venues that will take bookings and have credit card/EFTPOS charging facilities can save you a lot of hassle. They charge a ticket handling fee (in the vicinity

of two dollars per ticket), but if you have control of ticket prices, you can simply add this on to what you want to take per ticket. The venue should pass credit card fees on to the customer.

● Technical facilities and hands-on help—get a copy of the technical specifications and talk with designers about lighting and sound needs before booking the venue. Take your technical representative to the space and get them to make sure that everything on the list is in working order. Check out bump-in/out expectations and whether you can bring in any additional equipment that you need. More expensive venues often include a hands-on technical manager during bump-in and/or a technical operator. It is worth the extra money. If no operator is supplied, then ascertain the level of support you'll receive during bump-in and the kind of responsibility you have for the venue and its equipment. If you are working in a no-frills venue, check for three-phase power capability and the costs of bringing in your own lighting and sound rig. It's also worth asking if you have access to any set, costume or props stores.

● Front of House and cleaning services—does the venue run a bar and supply an usher? If not, you will have to find someone to sell tickets and manage the venue. Audiences expect to be able to buy drinks and snacks at interval; operating a bar and snack service with co-op resources is time-consuming but if it's run well it can be profitable. If you are selling alcohol you will need a temporary licence from your state or territory's liquor licencing authority [W10]. Don't forget to ask about the regularity of cleaning services for the foyer, theatre and backstage.

● Marketing and publicity—most HFH will expect companies to take care of their own promotional needs, but it's worth checking if there are newsletters, e-letters or planned mailouts to patrons that you can access.

- Company amenities—is there a small greenroom for actors? Are there clean toilets and a kitchenette? An on-site laundry is very handy for stage management, particularly if it's a high maintenance show.
- Other requirements—are you contractually obliged to advertise the show in the daily newspaper or have signs/billboards painted at your expense?

Getting it right with rights

The term 'copyright' literally means 'right to copy'. It refers to a creator's exclusive right to control the performance, reproduction or distribution of their work. Copyright law is an enormously complex area, but the basic rule of thumb is that if you can read, hear or watch it, you should assume that it's in copyright, unless you know it is in the 'public domain'—more on this later. Put simply, this means that *before* you commence rehearsals you need to get permission to perform the work from the creator, usually via a licensing agent. This is true both for scripts and any other material you wish to include, such as a song. Using scripts, music or recorded material without 'getting the rights' is a serious offence which can generate nasty penalties, regardless of how well or badly resourced your company may be, and whether or not it has amateur or professional status. In the eyes of the law copyright is property and using it without permission is theft.

Let's look at the very basic rights issues, the most likely scenarios that small independent companies will face. There are some key organisations that maintain informative websites that will help you gain an understanding of copyright law, such as the Australian Copyright Council [W11] and Arts Law [W12]. If you are in any doubt about whether you are doing the right thing, check it out thoroughly before proceeding.

Sean Lynch, Julia Davis, Gwyneth Price, Johnny Nasser and Benedict Hardie in the State of Play production of *Wilde Tales* for B Sharp. Photo: Brett Boardman

Playscripts

Once you have found a play you want to perform, the first thing you should do is to secure the performance rights. Get going with this before you start comparing rehearsal spaces and venues. If you have a printed copy of the script it should identify the agent who manages the rights. Otherwise, do a little web research and contact the writer's agent, who will be able to put you on the right track. If one of your collaborators has written the play or you are a close associate of the writer, then you'll be able to deal directly.

Essentially there are two types of rights that concern you, professional and amateur. Once professional seasons of a new play are finished, writers may choose to release amateur rights. The basic differences for a licensing agent are the amounts of money involved, the length of the season (professional seasons are generally longer) and whether the creative team is being employed. The major difference from a company's perspective is that professional rights are exclusive (for a particular geographical area), whilst most amateur rights are not. The geographical area is specified in the rights. If a company has secured exclusive professional rights in your state, you won't be able to get amateur rights to perform the work before they have finished with it. So if the company plans to tour, don't expect rights to become available for some time. Most unfunded independent companies apply for non-exclusive amateur rights, particularly for older works; they are cheaper (you can sometimes negotiate a 'per show' fee) and royalty advances are not as large. Bear in mind, though, that another independent company in your area can also pick up the non-exclusive rights to perform the play, possibly just before, or even at the same time as your season. Licensing agents should advise you of this if you enquire about it, but don't expect them to offer the information voluntarily!

How long it will take to negotiate the rights, and how successful you will be, depends on a number of factors including availability, the attitudes of the agent and writer toward co-operative work, the credibility of the team and presenting venue, and the performance history of the work. Generally speaking, the more recent the work and the hotter the playwright, the harder it will be. If you're itching to present a new international work that sold out in London last year, you will most likely find yourself competing with bigger companies and the agent will be looking to secure a fully professional production. You could be lucky enough to secure these rights, but the advance may be hefty.

If you're presenting something from the 1960s, the process should be much quicker, but this will not always be the case! Big companies often present revivals and if they have secured professional rights for the production, you'll be out of luck. Never assume that rights for any play will be easy to obtain.

The best weapon you can arm yourself with (apart from building a credible team and securing a good venue) is time. Give yourself plenty of it ... and then some! In the first instance, fax or email the agent to express your interest. Some licensing agents have application forms on their websites that you can submit electronically. If you suspect the rights may be restricted in some way, a quick phone call to check their availability isn't a bad idea. When you apply formally, agents will want to know the identity of the venue and its seating capacity (or projected audience attendance), the number of performances, average ticket prices and proposed opening and closing dates. If you are an unfunded company in a competitive situation and you want to strengthen your application, send a brief profile of the company with any good reviews or media coverage for previous shows and supporting letters. The agent will calculate an advance royalty fee (usually projected audience x average ticket price x number of performances x a set percentage, which for amateur rights is generally 10%). You will have to pay this upfront as a guarantee against 10% of box office income, with the greater sum becoming the final fee. Some agents won't make you pay an advance, but will set a minimum fee per performance against 10% of box office income. In the end you will pay whichever is greater.

I imagine there are a few hands raised at this point! How, may you ask, do I confirm the venue with the agent, when the venue won't finalise the booking until the rights are confirmed? You don't always have to wait for the other; in your initial approach you can indicate to the licensing agent that you are negotiating with Company X for a hiring or curated slot and update the agent as soon as your venue is in the bag. Many co-op negotiations, however, do find themselves faced with a dreaded chicken-egg scenario. There's no easy solution. You must juggle both of them skilfully until one or the other falls from the sky into the coop. Start with the rights and try to get as clear an idea as possible about whether you have a decent shot at them. If the agent is telling you that there are no other interested parties and that it looks pretty clear, or that you are the preferred party, but they want the venue confirmed and a couple of bits and pieces clarified, then you can at least say to the venue or season that you just need the commitment from them to wrap things up. At the same time you'll be ascertaining whether the venue is available and if the manager or curator is really interested in the play. If it's a sought after piece and the venue is dribbling over it a bit, you can be very positive with the agent. If you're in danger of losing one or the other because everyone is dawdling, apply pressure wherever you think it will have the most effect.

Juggling in the chook pen is one thing, lying is another. Never confirm one to the other when you don't really have the go-ahead— you don't want to end up with egg on your face. If you're going for a curated berth with a script for which there is huge competition, it's going to be harder again! Many curators simply will not program a new work unless the rights are absolutely confirmed.

There are more reasons to give yourself plenty of time to negotiate rights. It's very common for busy international agents to lose track of faxes and emails and significant time differences are unhelpful when you are trying to have a meaningful conversation with them. Arm yourself with patience, particularly if the play is hot property. Many small companies feel royally dicked around by this often lengthy process, as agents sound out and juggle options for the playwright. You may never get a reply no matter how many messages you leave, or wait ages for one. Be dogged but polite. Remember that agents are often waiting on answers themselves and their job is to get the best outcome for their client.

While this may sound like tough going, it is possible for good independent teams to nab premiere rights for hot scripts. There are some wonderful contemporary 'boutique' plays that generate a lot of initial interest and get temporarily vacuumed up by mainstream companies, who pay to hang on to the rights but decide against a production. Exciting works deemed too controversial or 'small' can get thrown back into the sea where, despite a lot of shark-circling by funded outfits, they remain unconsumed. Such strong works are often a perfect match for good independent companies working in intimate venues! Even if you give up on the rights and select another play, it might be worth revisiting them at a later date. Interesting co-op teams attached to good venues can be an attractive option for licensing agents who have been unable to secure mainstream productions for their client's work; strongly curated seasons now have a great deal of credibility both in Australia and overseas. It may take time, and the agent may have to double check with the writer, but many small companies have successfully secured rights to fantastic new plays. It's worth having a go, no matter how hopeless it seems at first.

A word of warning here about indie companies and 'professional' status. Whilst UK agents seem to have a good grasp of the curated independent scene in Australia, other international agents, particularly American outfits, do not. Some small companies I know have fallen foul of their own cheery explanations of Australian 'professional co-op' to New York agents. Their assurances to agents that their work is of the very highest standard, have elicited requests for hefty advances from agents who assume they are cashed up. If you are communicating with the agent via email or fax, provide a little background on your local independent theatre scene, the venue or season hub you are working in, and how your company fits into it.

The good news for independent theatre producers is that copyright does have a shelf life. In Australia copyright used to last until 50 years after the death of the creator (or, to get very technical, 50 years after the first performance if that happened after the author's death), and this is still true for writers who died in 1954 or earlier. However, with the advent of the US Free Trade Agreement, copyright has been extended to 70 years after the death of the creator, bringing us into line with America and Europe. (This means that while you can produce the work of a writer who died on 30 December 1954 without permission, you will need to wait until 2026 to produce the work of someone who died on 1 January 1955.)

If you want a little break from the melée, you might choose to produce works where copyright has expired and are now in the *public domain*. There are a huge range of works in the public domain from Greek tragedies, through Shakespeare and Jacobean works, from Molière through to Oscar Wilde. Oddly, the plays of Bernard Shaw, who died in 1950, are in the public domain in Australia, but not in the UK where copyright will last until 2021.

Producers still need to be very careful and check thoroughly before assuming a work is in the public domain. Many *translations* and *reworkings* of classic plays have been created by people who are still in copyright. If you have a funky translation of Molière or, say, a new adaptation of *Hedda Gabler*, at the front of the publication you will see how to apply for the rights to perform this particular *translation* or *adaptation*. Don't assume that *every* play from the early twentieth century is in the public domain. Some writers have long and distinguished writing careers and copyright dates from the death of the author, not the year the work was written.

Copyright protection for playwrights not only dictates whether a company can perform a work, but can set limitations on how they do so. There are some common misconceptions about exactly what kind of alterations, changes or deletions a company can make to a text. Some agents, authors and estates are particularly vigilant about this. They differ as to what is viewed as breaching copyright by misrepresenting the work, but generally you will be treading on dangerous ground if you:

- Edit the text in *any way* without written permission (this includes cutting or adding words, songs etc).
- Change the order of scenes.
- Fiddle with the gender of characters.
- Disregard stage directions (scary but true).
- Video performances without written permission, even for archival purposes (even scarier, but just as true).

It's probably obvious to you which actions are most likely to attract attention and trouble, but it's very important that you are aware of all breaches you might accidentally make in the name of contemporary art. It's generally accepted that older plays will be subject to re-interpretation for which original stage directions are no longer relevant, but this is not always the case. In 2002, Company B made front page news when Edmund Beckett challenged director Neil Armfield's use of music in his production of *Waiting for Godot*. Although the issue was resolved in Company B's favour, it was a highly charged incident for all involved. When it comes to playscript copyright you really need to carefully research every production on a case-by-case basis and read the rights contract *carefully* before signing it. In their dispute with the Beckett estate, Company B won out because their contract did allow for the use of music.

Music

Music rights are regularly misinterpreted, breached and botched by the independent theatre sector. Sometimes this happens through ignorance; but at other times companies wilfully bank on a 'blind eye'. In a nutshell, it isn't worth the risk of using music without obtaining the correct *form of rights*, particularly in a major city centre. If playscript licensing agents are vigilant, music licensing agents are ferocious. Big organisations will have no hesitation in closing down your production and suing you, regardless of how desperately poor you may be. If you're trespassing on heavily-guarded territory such as the Elvis estate, expect to lose your house and first born in the proceedings. In the past few years I have witnessed several productions threatened with serious legal action and shows closed down in production week which has caused a great deal of heartbreak and a lot of wasted money. Emerging theatremakers are often indignant about the rights of established playwrights and musicians, but it's important to value the work of other artists and remember that agents have a duty to protect it. You will be very thankful for such vigilance if, after years of slogging it out, you start to earn royalties yourself.

While music copyright has many forms, for the most part, independent companies will deal with rights for music *in dramatic context*. Dramatic context performance rights are different from those you would need if you were staging a musical (grand rights) or if you are just performing a bunch of songs in a cabaret or gig setting (small rights). It's much easier to obtain small rights, because the presentation doesn't manipulate the context of the music. Once you add a script, design elements and 'acting', you are using the work in a new context, and the author may not agree with it. Composers have the right to object to their work being associated with products or campaigns, and to determine if it can be used in a production to underline a point or generate a mood that reflects someone else's agenda or point of view. It doesn't matter if the music is being used to underscore a scene or for a more general purpose such as scene changes. Once the lights go down at the start of the performance, it is deemed to be in dramatic context.

You can apply to use specific songs or music for a performance by contacting the Australasian Performing Rights Association (APRA). They have an excellent website which explains music copyright in detail and you can apply for rights online [W13]. If APRA is not able to grant licences for certain songs or pieces of music, they will refer you to individual companies who can. Some publishers look after the rights for their clients directly.

Obtaining dramatic context rights for songs can take as long as getting playscript clearance, so give yourself heaps of time—at least eight to ten weeks. Many companies leave it far too late, and find opening night upon them with the rights still up in the air. You need that official piece of paper in your hand before you can go ahead. If a company finds out you have used unlicensed music in a performance—even if you eventually obtain approval—you can get yourself into hot water.

The same rules apply here as for original scripts and translations or re-workings: never assume that you will easily obtain the rights to use a piece of music or a song in dramatic context, no matter how old it may be. Even if a particular tune is in the public domain, the recording you use almost certainly won't be. It's safest to apply for all music and let APRA advise you of the work's status. And, again like scripts, you need specific permission for an archival recording of the performance. In recent years, a couple of companies who have altered lyrics to songs for satirical purposes were under the delusion that the work was not subject to copyright law because it had been 'changed'. In fact there is double damage here. You can neither alter the original song in any way without the author's permission, nor assume 'ownership' of the altered work. If you intend to perform music or a song 'live' in a scripted performance, you'll need to apply for rights in a dramatic context, even if one of the characters is simply whistling the tune as they walk through a scene.

Finally, check if the venue you are using has licences for playing incidental music in the foyer and theatres (before the show commences or after it has finished). All reputable venues will have appropriate licences through APRA and/or the Phonographic Performance Company of Australia (PPCA), which handles recorded music rights for such use. If you are working in a non-traditional space and you intend to play foyer music, you'll need to talk to PPCA, which also has an easily-navigated website with an online application facility [W14].

Insurances

It seems that every corner of our existence, both physical and otherwise, is now subject to the hovering spectre of insurance. Theatre-making hasn't escaped its gaze, and just because you may be working co-operatively doesn't mean you can avoid taking out some basic protection. You might be too poor to buy costumes, but insurance companies don't care; they'll sue the underpants off you if you engage in wrongful or negligent action.

Public Liability

In this litigious age, you'll be hard pressed to find a rehearsal room or venue that won't require your group to have its own Public Liability Insurance (PLI). Dramatic increases in insurance costs in the past couple of years have had a huge impact on the arts sector generally, with many companies and festivals being forced to scale back activities. For the indie sector the news isn't much better; some curated seasons have organised additional coverage for the small companies who work there, to make their venues more accessible, but most co-ops now have to bite the PLI bullet.

PLI relates directly to 'the public'. It provides cover for damages and injuries to members of the general public and their property, that may be caused by the company or a company member. For example, if an actor treads on a patron's foot during a performance and breaks the patron's toes, or a light falls from the rigging and hits someone, PLI pays for legal expenses and any damages. It does not cover company members who may be injured or lose property, however, nor does it grant the company a licence to behave irresponsibly. If you don't take reasonable (and legally required) precautions to protect the public, you may find that not only have you breached your policy agreement, but you are facing criminal charges.

If you are only mounting one show during the year, you'll need to purchase PLI for a single production, which is the most expensive way to buy cover. If you are planning a few activities for a year, which may include productions, general workshopping and class activities, it's well worth investigating associations who have set up group purchasing arrangements. These organisations have negotiated significantly cheaper insurance for not-for-profit companies engaged in similar (and often community-based) activities. The Association of Community Theatre **[W15]** and Duck for Cover (geared towards solo performers and musicians) **[W16]** are two such organisations. By joining, you can take advantage of negotiated rates that over a year can save you heaps of money. $1000–$1500 may sound like a lot of dough up front, but if you are mounting two or three productions and workshops, it's much more economical than a one-off purchase. If you are considering this, it's important to plan early as most of these group policies have defined dates for the start and end of coverage; if the cover ends on 31 December and you join on 31 November, you'll only get one month's coverage. These group policies don't cover the needs of all projects and it's important that you compare a few policies and read the fine print, so that you are absolutely sure of inclusions and exclusions. 'Our Community' has an excellent website for community organisations **[W17]**. It contains detailed information about where you can purchase public liability for not-for-profit ventures in all states. Arts Law **[W12]** has useful information sheets on its website and the National Insurance Brokers Association has an online database of brokers who deal with a range of insurances **[W18]**. It's also worth talking to season hub producers and indie-friendly venues for information about their own policies and brokers.

Other insurances

Funded productions must remunerate artists, crew and designers according to industry awards. As 'employers' you will be required by law to take out Worker's Compensation Insurance (WCI), which you will have factored into your funding applications for the duration of the project. If you haven't had to deal with this before, 'Workcover' websites specific to your state or territory are a good place to start gathering information **[W19]**. WCI isn't essential for co-op productions, however, since no-one is being employed (though some venues make this a condition of hire or entry to their season). This is one reason why Letters of Agreement are vital, and they should clearly state the relationship between all parties (profit-share, 'no employer'). If someone gets hurt and attempts to claim against 'the company' or producer, a co-op agreement signed by all parties can nip nasty legal shenanigans in the bud. Individuals should consider taking out personal insurance for themselves, particularly if the work is physically risk-taking.

Most co-ops don't bother with property insurance, but if you are borrowing or hiring expensive items such as musical instruments and video projectors, it's wise to think about it, and some equipment hiring companies may insist on it. If you don't have a legal business structure, though, you may find it hard to buy ad-hoc property insurance. See if someone in your company or the venue itself is willing to extend their existing personal or business policies to cover expensive items while they are in the rehearsal room or venue.

Any permits or licences that may be required for rigging, use of fire, pyrotechnics or hazardous substances should also be investigated during these early planning stages. We'll look at that in more detail when we address production week and risk-assessment in Chapter 9.

❸

Blueprinting

Schedules and company communication, money and budgets

Your show has been included in a season, or you have found the perfect venue to hire. Congratulations! Before you really start to cook up your show, however, there's some preparation to do. Think of the project as a ten course banquet—there are tasks such as shopping and lugging bags, weighing ingredients, chopping and marinating before you even begin to think of heating up the pan. Although you may be dead keen to dive in and start rehearsing, your show will have a much greater chance of success if the team gives itself sufficient time to plan all stages of the venture.

You should already have done some financial calculations and have seeding money in place. This is the starting point for organisational success, the blueprinting of your production.

However tedious it may seem, scheduling can save the team a lot of stress and strife, particularly when things start to heat up in the final stages of a project. If the team feels overwhelmed, it can refer back to these basic documents to look for gaps in communication or action, and to get back on track when things have gone off the rails. Scheduling provides a recipe for the big cook-up; you can add extras here and there when needed, but if you ditch the main ingredients or get the timings all wrong, you could end up with an indigestible mess. In short, good scheduling helps protect your two most precious resources—time and money.

I suggest that the company creates three minor blueprints—Rehearsal, Production and Technical, Marketing—and two major blueprints. The first major is your Budget (which you will already have sketched out), and the second the Producer Overview—the one true schedule to rule them all! In this section we deal with the major blueprints; we'll get down to subsidiary ones in their relevant chapters.

Major Blueprint One: Production Budget

The Producer should devise a production budget before anyone starts spending money. The expenditure column should include everything from venue and rehearsal costs, rights payments, marketing and publicity, set, props and costumes, bump-in costs through to post-show cleaning, set disposal and celebrations. Income is comprised of box office income (BOI) and the money you have in hand including personal donations or 'loans' from team members, grant monies and sponsorship both cash and in-kind. Schedule 2 shows a sample budget.

The first rule of thumb is to be realistic in your budgeting. There's no point in keeping your expenditure to a minimum on paper, if it's not achievable. As producer, you should create a draft budget, then meet with team members responsible for individual areas (such as your designers) and ascertain what they have in mind for the production. If your set designer simply has to cover the whole set in high maintenance white gloss paint, you may have to sacrifice something else. You'll have to negotiate with all members of your team, so that everyone understands exactly what resources will be lost in one area, when another is demanding more. Producers have the final call on budget allocations, since they will be the ones dealing with a nasty deficit at the end if things aren't managed responsibly.

SCHEDULE 2: Sample Production Budget

INCOME	Pebble Street Theatre (100 Seats)	
Box office	21 shows x $20 atp x 40%	$16,800
Programs	21 shows x 10 prog x $2	$420
Sponsorship—cash	Smith's Butchery	$1,000
TOTAL INCOME		**$18,220**

EXPENSES		
Venues		
Rehearsal	4 weeks x $100	$400
Theatre hire	4 weeks x $1,500	$6000
Insurances		
Public liability	$1000 for year (3 productions)	$335
Personnel		
Carpenter	Rostra build	$400
Production		
Set		$1000
Props		$250
Costumes		$500
Lighting	Equipment hire	$200
Sound	Consumables	$100
Ute hire	Bump in/out	$150
Marketing and publicity		
Design	Postcard, invitations and e-flyer	$250
Printing	Postcard and invitations	$1000
Distribution		$200
Postage	Invitations and offers	$300
Advertising	Street press	$250
Photography	Digital	$200
Publicity consumables	Mailing/faxing/couriers/kits	$300
Hospitality		
Opening night	Nibbles/champers	$200
Venue amenities	Coffee/tea/biccies	$50
Royalties		
Playwright	10% x $16,880	$1680
Music	1% x $16,800	$168
Archiving		
Video recording	Borrow camera/tapes	$20
Miscellaneous	Photos/cuttings	$50
TOTAL EXPENSES		**$14,003**
Plus contingency	10%	$15,403
PROFIT/LOSS		**$2817**

It is worth being tough at the start of proceedings so that everyone understands exactly how much can be spent in each area. If a team member finds something is more expensive than they first thought, they must seek approval before they commit to extra spending. As tough as it may sound, make a rule that any expenditure over the budget must be approved by the producer (in writing or by email) or borne personally by the spender! An email confirmation system is easy to manage and gives written records of the decisions.

Although you dream your show will be a runaway success, the financial fortunes of independent shows are extremely vulnerable. Mainstream professional companies have subscription seasons that effectively provide an audience for the first weeks of the season, and concurrently build word-of-mouth for when single tickets sales take over later in the season. As independent producers you rely almost totally on single ticket sales, the most difficult way to build audiences, since customer loyalty is transient at best. Your potential and often unknown audience will make snap decisions about your show, based on their exposure to marketing materials and strategies. The margin for success can be quite small, unless you have previously invested time and effort into audience development (more on this later).

It's imperative that you are truthful with yourself about the potential market for your show. It's almost impossible to predict accurately, but analysing the selling and anti-selling points will help you to be realistic. Take off your 'artist' hat for a moment and try and look at saleability from a general audience point of view. In some contexts, artistic excellence and talent will be the prime mover of tickets, but if you are really trying to get bums on seats from the general populace, you may find it's not the strongest selling point. Sadly, single ticket buyers will not necessarily flock to your show even if it's fantastic. Fabulous small-scale shows can get into a lot of financial difficulty if the anti-selling points haven't been taken into account in the financial planning and these dominate the public consciousness.

Don't get me wrong. It's imperative for your own development and the richness of the scene that you do the show you are passionate about, so take risks and challenge your audience to your heart's content. Just be realistic about drawcards and drawbacks when you are calculating box office income.

Selling points might be artistic excellence, the experience of the writer or devisers, the television and film profile of the actors, the size of the cast, the length of the play, the visibility of the venue, its relevance to current social and political issues and the artistic flavour of the production whether it be comic, confrontational, controversial, novel or quirky. If a show is perceived to be 'heavy', demanding, over long or in an uncomfortable venue, you'll need to work hard to overcome these points as 'anti-sellers', regardless of how good the production is. Similarly, a show with freshly-graduated performers will find it harder to get stories in the mainstream media, so take potential media coverage into account in your planning. Independent solo shows are always harder sells. So much depends on the brilliance of the performer and, because the artistic teams tend to have fewer members, their networks of personal contacts tend not to spread so widely.

Each production will have very different selling and anti-selling points, the nature of which will also be determined by location. As hard hearted (and unrelated to the art!) as some of these factors may seem, they inform the ticket-selling reality you'll face when pitching your show to the public.

So, what sort of percentages should you be looking at? Every show is different of course, but for a production in an intimate venue with a moderate-sized cast (five actors), it is common to budget for about 40% houses. If the cast is larger and the play well-known, you might

SCHEDULE 3: Sample Producer Overview

MARCH

Week 16
- Producer meeting #1
- Rehearsal room scout
- Venue scout
- Rights for script finalised

Week 15
- Investigate insurance options
- Draft list of potential sponsors

Week 14
- Draft of sponsorship document

Week 13
- Rehearsal room confirmed
- Venue confirmed

Week 12
- Producer meeting #2
- Insurances confirmed
- Sponsorship document signed off and circulated

APRIL

Week 11
- Design meeting #1

Week 10
- Design meeting #2

Week 9
- Publicity meeting #1

Week 8
- Producer meeting #3
- Promotional photo shoot
- Collect cast and crew biogs

- Sponsorship drive #2
- Draft company contact list

- Initiate weekly sales tracking system

MAY

Week 7
- Flyer artwork finalised

Week 6
- First read and design presentation
- Rehearsals commence
- Company contact list distributed
- Cast and crew producer briefing
- Media release finalised

Week 5
- Media release distributed

Week 4
- Flyers printed
- Flyers distributed
- Invitation lists finalised
- Finalise music rights

Week 3
- Opening night & preview invites mailed and emailled

JUNE

Week 2
- Technical plans finalised
- Media release re-distributed

Week 1
- Production week details finalised
- Catering organised

Production week
- Preview and opening finalised
- Production shots taken
- Media kits prepared
- Foyer boards prepared

Performance weeks
- Manage sales & guests
- Track marketing & publicity
- Attend to company needs
- Organise bump-out and celebration

aim for 50–60%; but if it's a newly developed solo show perhaps 30–35%. If you want to take selling points into account in a more rigorous manner, you could start with 40% and then add 2% for every selling point and subtract 3% for every anti-selling point. There are always 'difficult' shows that rise above the calculations, but there's no harm in budgeting modestly and enjoying a well-earned surplus at the end!

Major Blueprint Two: Producer Overview

This is a big picture document that allows quick reference to all the 'top and tail' points of major tasks and events as Schedule 3 shows. Keep it simple—no more than a page. You will have the opportunity to record detail in the minor blueprints, which will be more relevant to individuals with specific duties. The Overview blueprint can be circulated to everyone in your team, but primarily it helps the producer to keep track of the entire process.

Depending on the scale of your production, start the schedule between twenty and twelve weeks out (no less than eight weeks out is recommended) starting with initial tasks and working your way forward to opening night.

Company communication

Lots of really promising companies have gone by the wayside due to the effects of poor communication. If you ask collaborators why they 'broke up', they will say something like 'key members of the group keep making decisions about things that affect us all, without letting everyone know' or 'production weeks are always a nightmare 'cause no-one seems to know who's doing what'.

All collaborators have a responsibility to pass on information to the group where it's relevant, but if the producer establishes an effective communication system at the start of proceedings, it's safe to say that there'll be fewer stuff-ups and frayed nerves as the company heads toward the final stages of production. A good communication system should incorporate:

- A primary artistic contact and primary producing contact, who have final say in these areas. Until you have a publicity contact in place, the producer can handle any communication in this area.
- An emailable contact list that is *vigilantly* updated. Your first contact list should be drawn up and emailed the day the company commits to the project, and updated with each new participant. Everyone involved with the production should receive updates. Partners such as hired publicists and season curators should be sent the contact list once the majority of collaborators are on board.
- A phone and email relay system. Establish who has regular access to email and who is hard to contact by phone. If actors are doing other work during rehearsal periods and need to switch off their mobile phones, make sure they check for important messages when they can—it's very easy to miss a good publicity opportunity when someone is hard to contact. Establish contact 'networks' for each area of the production, mini email lists for passing on information. Who is responsible for letting the company know when rehearsal times have changed? Who needs to know about all aspects of the set build? If as producer you are wary of the communication abilities of the group, make yourself the central point for passing on information. You could set up an informal email report early on, with participants emailing the producer at the end of each week with updates about their production areas.
- Regular production meetings. We'll talk more about this in Chapter 9.

Schedule 4 outlines a simple communication chart for a co-operative production.

SCHEDULE 4: Sample Company Communication Chart

1. Rehearsals	All
2. Marketing	P, D, PU & GD
3. Production and design	P, PM, D, PD, SM & helpers
4. Finances	P, PM, PD
5. Publicity	P, PU, SM, D & C where relevant
6. Opening and sales	All
7. Design briefs	All
8. Publicity briefs	All

KEY

All: Whole company	**C**: Cast	**D**: Director
GD: Graphic designer	**P**: Producer	**PD**: Production designers
PM: Production manager	**SM**: Stage manager	**PU**: Publicist

Contracts and Letters of Agreement

During the critical planning and blueprinting stages, producers should put together a co-operative Letter of Agreement (LOA) for everyone who takes part in the production. Why is this so important? As discussed in Chapter 1, the legal vulnerability of individuals working on a co-op basis is a very real issue, and it's vital that a simple document is created that clearly outlines the relationship of company members (profit-share, 'no employer'), how the production is to be managed and details of the profit-share arrangement.

This LOA doesn't need to be filled with legal jargon and it really can be just a letter; keep it simple, but include everything that has been negotiated and agreed. If you have actors who are members of the Media and Entertainment Arts Alliance you can use their excellent standard Co-operative Agreement. It's a clear, simple document that can be adjusted according to any special needs.

Working without an agreement really isn't worth the risk; if anyone baulks at signing one without good cause, find someone else for the job (unless your proposed 'contract' is unfair in some way). Is it so hard to imagine an actor who is not part of the core team tripping on the set and twisting an ankle? Accidents, most of which are thankfully minor, happen all the time. What would you do if an actor (who doesn't consider himself a member of the company) demands the co-op cover him or her for expensive medical treatment or sues you for emotional trauma.

In the LOA, you can be clear with each other that personal accident insurance is the responsibility of the individual. Such documents won't stop someone trying to take legal action (and they may have a right to do so in the case of gross negligence), but you'll have a much better chance of defending yourself if you have a basic agreement in writing.

Profit-share

There are a number of ways to slice a profit-share egg; let's take a look at a common scenario.

'The Flying Pigs' have raised $2000 in cash sponsorship, and three of the core actors have decided to put in $2000 each to get the ball rolling. With $8000 in the bank, the company has enough for basic marketing/publicity and insurance costs, money for set and costumes and a deposit (first week's rent) for the venue. No-one else brought into the company for the production is required to make a financial contribution.

The production costs $10,000 to mount and brings in $22,000 (clear of GST and ticket handling fees). Once all expenditure has been tallied and balanced against income, those who have loaned money to the company are the first to be reimbursed. In this instance the three investing actors recoup their $2000 each, leaving $14,000 to be split amongst themselves and other co-op members. This money can be split evenly amongst everyone involved, or in some cases, co-op members may channel the profit back into a future production. When there is only a tiny profit, everyone may agree that it's more productive in the long-term than walking away with a few dollars each.

Where larger amounts of money are involved, or when the company has used mostly non-core collaborators, a more complex approach may be needed. As indie companies generate larger box-office income, a 'point system' has become a popular way of dealing with profit-share. Each collaborator is given a fixed number of profit points for their contribution. Perhaps the director, producer and actors receive 2 points, designers 1.5 points and general helpers .5 of a point. The producer adds the total number of points, calculates individual point percentages within the total point count, and then splits profit according to these percentages. Schedule 5 shows how this works for 'The Flying Pigs'.

SCHEDULE 5: Sample Profit Share of $14,000

ROLE	POINTS	% SHARE	$ SHARE
Producer	2	10%	$1400
Director	2	10%	$1400
Actor 1	2	10%	$1400
Actor 2	2	10%	$1400
Actor 3	2	10%	$1400
Production manager	2	10%	$1400
Set designer	2	10%	$1400
Stage manager	2	10%	$1400
Production co-ordinator	1	5%	$700
Sound designer	1.5	7.5%	$1050
Lighting designer	1.5	7.5%	$1050
TOTAL	20	100%	$14,000

The point system helps to recognise the differences in time commitment for individuals, but it can be very contentious, so it's important the system is thoroughly thrashed out by the company. If a sound design is a very small component of the production and is completed in two days, then it's reasonable for actors to want more profit points when they've committed to eight weeks of rehearsals and performances. Conversely, a designer may spend a huge amount of time preparing music or set and costume items; just because they are not working with the core team for the whole production period, does not mean their contribution is not equal to the producer, director and actors.

As with all important decisions, it's vital that the entire company has a thorough understanding of how and why they are made. Open lines of communication are the key to success.

More on money matters

If there is a legal business structure in place, then stringent financial control and reporting becomes part of the company's operations. The company must also deal responsibly with corporate governance (board or committee management) and the level of accountability this brings. You'll be audited annually, and if you are mounting several shows, touring and/or gaining funding, you'll need to invest in accounting software or the services of a bookkeeper to ensure things run smoothly.

If you are an unincorporated indie company mounting a show every now and then, you should be able to keep track of production income and expenditure and reconcile these using Excel which comes with every Microsoft Office package—even a really old version will do the trick. Excel lets you enter financial data and input formulas that will perform calculations as you go along. If you are not familiar with its features, work your way through its 'Help' section or visit the Microsoft website [W20], which provides access to informative online tutorials. You can also use this versatile program for creating, storing and sorting other types of information. For example you can collect names and addresses and perform mail merges allowing you to create form letters and labels for mailouts.

Once you have seeding money, you should open a bank account for the group or the production. All money can be handled through this account with the producer as sole signatory, or joint signatory for significant amounts, signing and distributing cheques as required. You need enough funds to cover invoices that must be paid before box office returns start to come in. Since it's inconvenient for the producer to give over small amounts of money continually, you may wish to set up petty cash arrangements for production managers and designers. Alternatively, ask them to keep receipts so they can be reimbursed.

Producers should gather receipts and invoices and reconcile petty cash on a regular basis. Don't leave this until the end of the production, as you'll have no idea where you're at. Expenditure should be entered daily into your spreadsheet and cash flow monitored carefully; if the budget looks as though it will blow out in one area, or your money is starting to dry up, you'll need to be aware of it sooner rather than later. Check out Tasmania's 'Arts Up' website [W21] which has a section on the practicalities of mounting a project, and includes a sample cash flow chart. Cash flow templates for small businesses can be downloaded from the Microsoft website [W20] but require some adapting.

Most venues will reconcile BOI on a weekly basis, so you will have access to income from the second week. You should get a weekly report generated through the venue's box office system; if you don't understand the layout or codes used, ask a member of the box office staff. A breakdown of 'buyer types' should be provided, showing the number of full price and concession tickets sold, tickets sold through deals and also complimentary tickets. Keep a careful eye on comp numbers; if they are significantly greater than you expect, you should investigate.

The producer takes responsibility for making sure outstanding bills are paid, including rights and royalties, and that the final box office reconciliation is complete and correct. They will then distribute any profit to company members, according to the agreed profit-share system. If the final result is a negative one, the core company and producer will need to meet immediately to talk about how outstanding debts will be managed. Remember that without a legal structure you are operating as a group of individuals, making you personally liable for any debts. The letter of agreement which everyone has signed should have clear instructions as to how to deal with a negative financial result.

Handling a company's production money is a big responsibility, but if you are methodical and vigilant, you should be able to head off small problems before they become big ones. Keep in close contact with your production manager and provide regular expenditure updates to designers. Encourage your colleagues to be responsible and careful with the company coffers.

ABNs and taxes

An Australian Business Number (ABN) identifies you or your company when dealing with the Australian Tax Office (ATO) and other government agencies. If you are a company, an individual or an entity carrying on an enterprise in Australia, you are entitled to an ABN. If you supply goods and services without providing an ABN, then payments to you may be subject to 48.5% withholding tax. This primarily impacts on indie companies in relation to government grants and box office income.

Until recently, it was common for individuals without an ABN to sign contracts with venues as 'hobbyists' in order to avoid withholding tax. There has always been a fine line here. Many people work in indie companies with professional interest, but the financial gain is so low that the activity could be classed as a recreational pursuit. Yet audiences for indie shows have grown (with box office income often exceeding the $20,000 mark), and more venues are demanding an ABN for contractual purposes. If you want to gain full possession of a government grant at the time you need it, or your full income at the end of the production, it's worth getting an ABN. It's easy to do: apply online as an individual or for a partnership or company with the Australian Business Register [W22].

Note that money earned and spent through a theatre production is considered the taxation responsibility of one or more individuals by the ATO, unless you have a formal structure in place. If a core member 'owns' the ABN for the company, then it makes sense that they sign contracts and open the account for the production. In this instance, that person would take financial responsibility for the production at tax time. One way of lessoning the tax impact on one person is to create an informal partnership with core members by applying for a partnership ABN. Production income is still dealt with on individual tax returns, but at least it is split between the partners.

An ABN also allows you to register for the Goods and Service Tax (GST), although it's not required if your annual turnover is less than $50,000. If you do register, you will have to charge 10% GST on any goods and services you offer (tickets for shows), although you will also be able to claim back the GST you pay on things you buy for the show ('input tax credits').

The downside of GST registration for indie operators is the administration and paperwork. You will need to collect the 10% GST on ticket sales for the ATO (and not be tempted to spend it!) and lodge a return (Business Activity Statement or BAS) on a monthly or quarterly basis. If you are going to spend enough on productions or equipment to make the claim for tax credits worth your while, then consider it. For unfunded indie companies who are just starting out, the administrative effort would certainly outweigh any benefit.

Bear in mind that GST also impacts on grants. Check procedures with your funding body before applying. As a general rule, applicants are required to include GST on requested amounts if they are not registered for it (since you will need to pay GST on goods and services you purchase) and exclude it if they are registered (funding bodies will pay GST in addition to the grant request). It's important to get this right if you don't want to be out of pocket, particularly when you are not registered and so unable to claim tax input credits.

The ATO **[W23]** has comprehensive online guides that explain the way income tax applies to individuals and not-for-profit companies, as well as information about GST and other taxes. Taxation is a complex area, so do some detailed research with the ATO or chat with an accountant.

4

Cooking up a show

Cast, crew and design

A production brings together a lot of individuals with differing opinions and agendas. The stimulus of arguing and bartering over issues is all part of the game, and if no-one was ever challenged, you'd probably end up with a boring product. Nevertheless, you want to avoid serious conflict; the sort that undermines the efficiency and enjoyment of everyone involved.

The producer or producers are in a brilliant position to oversee and unify the creative and production teams, and to get ideas flowing. Effective communication channels, good timing and a degree of like-mindedness amongst the major players are the keys to success.

Mess hall

Once a play has been selected and you have a fair idea who will be critically involved, the company will start discussing a basic vision for the production and how to build the best team to do it. It's helpful to have a general meeting of the core collaborators at this point, so that the director (and collaborator-designer if the team has one), can briefly explain what they have in mind for the project and what type of actors/crew/designers will be needed to achieve it. You don't need a lot of detail, but if the director has decided to relocate *Othello* to

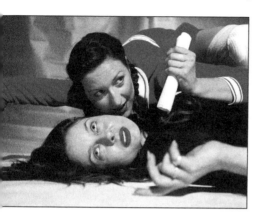

Kate Box and Rebecca Smee in the SMUGG Theatre production of *I've Got the Shakes* for Darlinghurst Theatre Company. Photo: Brett Boardman

the other side of the galaxy in the year 3005, it's important that the whole company knows this from the outset, and has the chance to express their opinion.

Once this sketch has been presented, the group can discuss whether to draw the cast from the core group and if any auditions are required. If someone suggests actor X or designer Y, other people who've worked with them or seen their work can offer their opinion. You may have your eye on a brilliant actor to supplement the group, but if they've been difficult to work with in co-op situations in the past or have an acrimonious relationship with one of the group, it's good to find out before you cast them. Perhaps someone in the group has seen a regional show with a great design and can throw a new contact into the pot.

You may be wondering if too many cooks will spoil your broth. There needs to be a 'final say' rule in place; everyone in the company should contribute what they know, based on their experience and professional friendships, so long as it's understood that 'final say' rests with the producer, director or artistic director. But if 99% of the company is opposed to wearing silver body paint and carrying laser guns for *Othello*, then the director should probably reconsider the play or the vision for it!

Ideally, this first core collaborator meeting should take place 4–5 months out and kick-start an ongoing discussion of issues such as:

- Production roles (marketing, publicity etc)
- Casting and auditions, other creative roles
- Production management and crewing
- Funds—ballpark budgets and fundraising

Casting

Once you have cast the core collaborators, most likely you'll be looking for actors for other roles. You may be familiar with them because you have seen them in co-op productions or they have worked with members of the company in other collaborations. During the company meeting, you may also come up with actor/s with a higher professional profile, that you think might be interested in a really juicy role, especially if your company has a strong reputation for excellent work. The artistic standard of the independent scene has risen dramatically in the past five years, and while many artists once swore they would never 'do co-op', some experienced actors are now realising that they can often find the interesting and risk-taking roles they seek on the independent scene. It's now quite common for indie companies to approach higher-profile actors or their agents, particularly if they are looking for a 'specialist' actor (of age, ethnicity, physical stature etc). It pays to be realistic about such approaches though—if it's your first production and the play is nothing special, then you probably won't get past first base. But for a company with a good track record, an up-and-coming director and a hot script, it's absolutely worth a go.

The actor's agent will initially want to know the identity and background of key collaborators, such as the director and other actors, in addition to basic information such as venue and dates. If it's a large agency, make a quick call to find out the specific person there who represents the actor. If the actor is technically available and the agent is interested, send the agent any information they want along with the most up-to-date script and negotiate from there. Some agencies are also amenable to broader requests from non-funded indie companies. If you are seeking an actor for a specialist role, then send information to agents, and ask them to send suitable actors to audition. If you're going to try this approach, it's best to do a little research first. Get your hands on a copy of Showcast [W24] or subscribe to its online service to gain a better knowledge of representation. Agents won't be impressed if you know nothing about their clients or if you contact them with a list of general roles and no real idea of who or what you are looking for. They may not be interested in digging through their files of twenty-somethings for a role that could easily be cast within your own networks, but may be very eager to connect you with an older or ethnic client for a unique character in a special play. East Coast Theatre Company's unfunded production of *The Empress of China* for B Sharp was greatly assisted by the goodwill of Sydney agents and casting directors and the company secured eight terrific Asian actors.

An obvious source of great new talent is acting schools. Almost every institution has an annual graduate showcase between October and December and it's worth at least one person taking time to attend, or split sessions amongst members. Contact schools mid-year to see if dates and venues have been confirmed or ask to be put on a mailing or invitation list. Most schools have packs of photos and CVs that you can take away with you on the day. Check too for the myriad of showcase productions throughout the year that are regular features of acting school calendars.

Open auditions are very time-consuming and I wouldn't recommend them if you have halfway decent networks in the core group. In terms of unearthing great new talent, expect about a 5% return on a considerable investment of time and labour. There are also some very 'professional auditioners' out there; actors who'll knock your socks off with their monologue work, and promptly fall apart during an intensive rehearsal process or a performance run. If you want to go the open audition route, though, advertise in the street press, or post notices through email networks, on acting school or indie venue noticeboards. Arts Hub **[W25]** is an excellent online service for arts workers that will allow you to post notice of auditions. An annual subscription fee gives access to a comprehensive arts jobs information service, and their independent arts news outlet. There are some theatre websites that also include auditions such as Theatre Australia **[W26]**. A good alternative to advertising is to run a regular workshop that includes artists from outside the core group. Why not set-up 'open' workshops for all comers, or invite promising people to join you for a few sessions so that you can get to know them and see how they work in a group situation?

Regardless of how you source actors, it's essential to find out about their performing history before you take them on. If no-one in the group has personally worked with them, find someone who has and do a discreet 'reference check'.

A few words regarding 'availability'. The hotter the actor and the more experience they have in television and film, the greater the risk they will be offered a paying gig after committing to your project. This is a tricky thing, as no-one wants an actor to miss out on an amazing opportunity. Strictly speaking, agents shouldn't put actors up for projects when they are already spoken for even if the commitment is to an indie show, but many would consider they weren't doing their best for their clients if they knocked back an audition for a prestigious and well-paid job. Before committing to actors in this position, the producer and director should talk candidly with them about how availability should be handled. It's quite common for actors to need rehearsal days off for ads and series work; most indie companies work around these obstacles. It's quite another thing for an actor to make themselves significantly unavailable for rehearsals or to interfere with scheduled performances. The company should discuss the parameters of additional work; it's really up to individual actors to brief their agents about what may or may not be possible (and to be honest with you about it!).

In the end, it's entirely acceptable for a small company with professional interests investing a significant amount of time, effort and money to expect the best work and commitment possible from all actors. Season-based venues often program with the match of material and cast in mind and curators can get pretty annoyed if the promised team falls apart. At the very least you should demand total commitment after a certain date; if the actor disregards this promise and pulls out after the agreed cut-off point, you have every right to accuse them of professional disrespect. Some actors may find this suggestion offensive, but independent theatre is now regarded by industry as a credible professional forum for artists. Many actors have benefited professionally from indie gigs and it's only fair that work at this level be treated with respect by anyone who hopes to benefit from it again.

Crewing

Theatre training institutions in Australia turn out a high proportion of top-notch technical and production graduates. Although a lot of them get snapped up by professional companies, many also enjoy working on the indie scene. There is often considerable attraction for them in maintaining links with fellow graduates from other disciplines, and being part of small companies that give them more of a say in what goes on. If you can incorporate one or two great techies or stage managers into the core of your group then you're cooking with gas! Good production people diversify and increase the company's skills base and provide invaluable creative and practical advice.

If you were running a fully professional company you might have a vast team of people such as a production manager, technical managers, mechanists, stage managers and assistants, costume co-ordinators, builders and so on. The more task-specific people you can build into your team the better, but most companies don't need (and don't have!) a dozen people to get a small-scale production up and running. Most indie companies are lucky to have a set designer and one person to run around and co-ordinate everything. Some designers are more hands-on than others; if they can also sew and have building experience it's a bonus! The best-case scenario for a small co-op production would probably be individual set, costume, sound, lighting and media designers combined with:

- Production Manager: gathers venue plans and technical specifications and keeps the venue's technical manager up-to-date regarding show specific plans. Works with designers to budget, plan, schedule, source and build. Liaises with stage manager and producer, and oversees the whole production process including bump-in/out.

- Stage Manager: works closely with the director, manages rehearsal room activities, notes blocking and requests, schedules rehearsals and changes, liaises with publicist, maintains contact lists, liaises with production manager about what is needed. In a performance run, usually calls lights and sound, manages cast and crew, gives pre-show calls, sets stage for performances.

- Production assistants: A volunteer attached to each designer and the production manager to help gather props, costumes and materials, build and rig lights.

Of course not every company will have the 'luxury' of a production manager and a stage manager for both rehearsals and performances. In co-op situations these roles often get modified in very creative ways! It can be done, but if you are working with few resources, you have to plan carefully, be clear with everyone about their individual responsibilities and make sure that all bases are comfortably covered, particularly during production week. If you have very hands-on set and costume designers who can source and make as well as devise, then you might be able to make do with a couple of helpers during production week, in lieu of an experienced production manager. If the curated season you are part of supplies a Technical or Stage Manager for the performance run, then you may be able to do without a stage manager for a small production. In these cases the designated producer might also step in to fill in some of the gaps, such as helping to service the rehearsal room and co-ordinate production week.

At the very least you need to have one production person (designer, production manager or stage manager) to 'service' the rehearsal and make sure that the creative team has basic props etc, and to source and prepare for production. For production week you will need two *supervising* production people (aside from lx/sfx designers) that are in the venue 80% of the time; a hands-on set designer, production manager or helper who is very handy with a drill and hammer and can supervise the build during production week, and a stage manager or helper to liaise with actors, set up dressing rooms and deal with smaller production tasks. There should be at least one other helper to run around and pick up last-minute items, so that everyone else can work continuously in the venue. Depending on the scale of the production, you may also need two to three extra helpers to assist with building and rigging.

Schedule 6 shows three examples of the many co-op production team combinations I have seen in action. Scenario A is well-resourced, B moderately so, and C is a bare-bones option. Scenario C is really only suitable for very small-scale productions (solo and 2-handers), with minimal makes and builds.

SCHEDULE 6: Sample Production Team Combinations

	SCENARIO A	SCENARIO B	SCENARIO C
Rehearsal room	Production manager Stage manager	Stage manager Designer	Designer Producer
Pre-production sourcing/ Builds	Designers (2–4) Production manager 1 helper	Designers (1–3) Production manager	Designer Producer 1 helper
Production week	Designers (2–4) Production manager Stage manager Operator/Technician 2 helpers	Designers (1–3) Production manager Operator/Stage manager 1 helper	Designer 2 helpers
Performance run	Stage manager Operator/Technician	Operator/Stage manager	Operator/ technician
Bump-out/Post-production	Designers (2–4) Stage manager 2 helpers Operator/Technician	Designers Production manager 1 helper	Designer Producer 2 helpers

Design

Talented and resourceful designers can be thin on the ground in the indie scene, but designers who achieve wonders in small spaces do exist and have significantly raised the design bar in recent years. If you are applying to a season hub, you'll need to demonstrate that your company can handle the design demands of the show and maximize the use of space.

In some companies the design process is very organic, with designers working during the rehearsal period and responding to artistic choices as they evolve. This is a wonderful way to work, but for unfunded companies often it is neither possible nor suitable for every type of project.

For most text-based projects, discussions of the set design should start as early as possible (see Schedule 3 on page 58). The director and designer (and costume designer if they are separate) can begin knocking around ideas as soon as the project is on the table, meeting casually to discuss themes, evolving directorial vision, colour and textures. It's helpful for all parties to bring physical things along to help tease out ideas. Books, magazine pictures, works of art and colour charts are all great tools for demonstrating to each other what's floating around in your heads. Words don't always suffice when you are dealing with shapes, textures and hues.

The designer/s can present sketches in subsequent meetings, and the Producer and Production Manager can be brought in as the design takes shape, to discuss scheduling and cost issues. All four parties should work together to ensure a wonderful and, most importantly, achievable design. Whilst everyone will want to serve the creative vision of the show, if the Producer or Production Manager has concerns about cost, or the group's ability to manage the set-build during the bump-in period, they have every right to request a discussion, and perhaps modifications to the design. A fabulous set shouldn't be at the expense of the time needed to tech the show properly and to give actors and the director the chance to segue comfortably from the tech period to dress rehearsal to preview and opening. I've seen many groups get themselves into hot water when it's too late to cool things down; someone should speak up at an earlier stage if they feel the director and designer are over-ambitious.

Sound and lighting designs generally come together during the rehearsal period. A composer, if one is involved, will liaise with the director over a longer period, so the pair can work out compositional needs between them. The composer may supply sound bites or samples, which can be tried out in rehearsal between or under scenes.

All designers work in different ways, but it's important for the producer to ensure that samples get to the rehearsal room when needed and that delivery dates for final designs and music are understood and agreed. A lighting designer should have a rough lighting plan sorted out about two weeks out from bump-in (and a more fully refined one after seeing runs in the final week of rehearsals), and any sound discs that will be used during the show, must be ready for scheduled technical rehearsals.

It's important that the stage manager, or whoever is responsible for creating rehearsal schedules, builds time into the schedule for measuring the cast and fitting costumes, since these can usually only be done once rehearsals are underway.

The producer of a small unfunded project is wise to negotiate delivery dates with all designers and to maintain regular contact with everyone. If a designer looks as though they are getting behind, you have a much better chance of helping and solving the problem when things start to slide, rather than at the eleventh hour, when it's painfully obvious there will be no music or sound effects for the first technical rehearsal.

A danger point for a blow-out in the design budget is during bump-in week, when things don't always go according to plan. Suddenly you find that you need more expensive paint, floor sealer or hired equipment. Even with the best planning, it's hard to avoid hiccups. It's a good idea to factor in a contingency of around 10% when budgeting, to help deal with any small oversights or emergencies.

First rehearsals

Everyone involved with the production should be at your first rehearsal or 'read'. It's one of the few opportunities you will have to share ideas and plans for the show together. First reads are joyful occasions and help to create a sense of excitement and enthusiasm for the group journey you are about to embark on.

Once the team has gathered over coffee and a sticky bun, the producer and/or director should make introductions and outline each person's role.

It's vital that a co-op producer has an opportunity to talk to the whole team about budgets, contracts or letters of agreement and general 'group-effort' expectations early in the proceedings. Ideally this is done in a separate meeting before the first rehearsal, but if it's difficult to get everyone together, the first read may be your only chance to run through the basics. Get it out of the way after introductions. Save time by preparing an A4 sheet that clearly outlines the budget, details profit-share arrangements and any extra duties that may be required (leaflet distribution, prop and costume sourcing) and brief notes about timeliness, tidying up issues and contact procedures for rehearsal lateness or in the case of illness. Contracts or Letters of Agreement should have been circulated prior to the first rehearsal, and if they are not returned at the rehearsal, then set a strict deadline for this. Finally, circulate the most up-to-date contact list and ask everyone to check for changes or errors.

The director and stage manager usually work together to create a rehearsal schedule (see Schedule 7, page 83), with the stage manager breaking the play down into scenes or even smaller chunks of text or action. If the director likes to work in a very particular or non-sequential way, they may choose to break the play down themselves, building in short periods for specific exercises or group work. In such cases the stage manager should ensure that time for costume fittings, design updates, photo sessions and production meetings (once a week is desirable) are plotted into the schedule. If you are creating a devised or physical work, it's vital that clear schedules are produced. Whilst you are building structure rather than deconstructing it, it's important to plot in key points in the devising journey; this is easier if you've already completed a creative development phase and have a clear sense of direction for the piece.

If you are lucky enough to have a creative team that can rehearse through the day without too much interruption, then you'll have the luxury of creating a full rehearsal schedule. This, of course, is the best case scenario, the worst being working around actors on a daily basis, constantly changing the schedule and managing time-consuming phone updates. At the very least, you should expect time commitments from the director and actors for a week at a time. It's a good idea to encourage a regular pattern where everyone updates the stage manager as to availability on a Friday, so that on Saturday the following week's schedule can be emailed to the whole company.

When reading the play for the first time, it's helpful if the director relaxes the cast by encouraging them to take it slowly and read naturally at a conversational volume, resisting the urge to 'perform'. Actors can be very nervous at a first read and shouldn't be forced or embarrassed into delivering a perfect accent or cracking pace in front of peers. The company has weeks to rehearse the show; the first read is an infant step on the journey to creative realisation, and shouldn't lock anyone into premature choices.

Many small productions don't bother with a formal design presentation, but I strongly advise you do so wherever possible. The designer may not be able to construct a model with moveable figures and miniature set items, but they can at least provide set plans to scale and sketches that show the use of structures, textures and colours. If you are working in an established venue, it's worth asking if there is an existing model box that can be borrowed.

Costume designers may not have swatches of fabrics to show, particularly if they are collecting costumes rather then making them, but sketches or pictures and photos that reflect their influences are a must. If 'collecting' props, costumes and set pieces is going to be a collaborative effort, pictures give everyone a clear indication of what to start looking for in op shops, garage sales or their own wardrobes.

The director may already have shared their ideas for the piece with key collaborators, but the first read is an excellent time to bring newcomers up to speed. The director could talk about mood and style, the use of the physical space, their method of breaking down text and what they are searching for physically and emotionally in exploring the work. Any preparatory requirements (accent work, warm-ups, research) should also be discussed. Sound and lighting designers and composers can also discuss how their work connects with the overall creative vision.

If you have a dedicated rehearsal space, it can be very useful for the designer/s to bring along books and magazines that capture the history, flavour and style of the piece (particularly if the show is set in another era or deals with other cultures) and leave them for browsing during rehearsals. Inspiring sketches, pictures and photos can be blue-tacked to walls or pinned to notice boards, transforming a hall-for-hire into a welcoming space for the production. Making a home for the company can work wonders for actors and directors who are have just finished a shift at the local cafe and need to shake off the outside world and embrace a more contemplative, creative one.

In relation to the production period, it pays to think ahead and be prepared. Producers should ensure that any paperwork is available for distribution at the first meeting and be confident enough to answer any questions about the company or production set-up. If your first read is conducted in the rehearsal room, ensure it is 'set-up' with all necessary amenities (coffee/tea, clean toilets, heating/lighting). It's a great way to make everyone confident in your artistically sensitive and fabulously organised producing team!

SCHEDULE 7: Rehearsal Schedule: *Terminus* (week 1)

DATE	TIME	AGENDA	REQUIRED	NOT AVAILABLE
Sat 22 Jan	10am–5pm	First read	Whole company	
Sun 23 Jan	X			
Mon 24 Jan	4.30pm–5.30pm	Discussion	Jenya & Joseph	Mark, Tom, Ben Jenya
	5.30pm–9pm	Discussion	Whole cast	leave at 6.45pm
Tues 25 Jan	4pm–9pm	Discussion	Whole cast	Tom, Ben leave at 8pm
Wed 26 Jan	X	Australia Day		
Thurs 27 Jan	9am–11am	Design meeting	Joseph, Steve, James, Sam,	
	11am–12pm	Mark up stage on rehearsal floor		
	2pm–5pm	Sc 4, Sc 15, Sc 22	John, Woman	
Fri 28 Jan	10am–1pm	Sc 3, Sc 9, Sc 16	Police Serg, Cop	
Sat 29 Jan	10am–1pm	Sc 21	Police Serg, Cop, Man	
	2pm–3.30pm	Sc 11, Sc 18	John, Man	
	3.30pm–5pm	Sc 6	Man, Cop	

Prepared by Sam Hawker for East Coast Theatre Company

5

Painting the town

Marketing that matters

At about the same time you're throwing all those tasty show elements into the pressure cooker, you'll be supervising the concoction of the next course: your masterful marketing plan.

You may think it's a waste of time to plan much of anything on a few dollars and cents, but if you follow some simple rules, you'll be surprised how much of a splash you can make on a tiny budget. You won't compete with the visiting international company spending thousands of dollars on glossy brochures and daily newspaper display ads, but hitting the right promotional chord at the epiphanic moment has very little to do with a fat wallet. There are many big-budget shows that fail to move tickets with a truck-load of advertising, and many little ones that have grabbed the attention of the public and media with an eye-catching image, tag-line or promotional hook. Independent companies can sometimes use the risk-taking aspects of their work to their advantage; nothing captures people's imaginations more than hot topicality, irreverence and controversy!

There are many websites and books on offer that give detailed and expert advice on planning and managing marketing campaigns. Of particular note for small companies is the Australia Council's [W27] fuel4arts.com website [W28], particularly its SAUCE section, which is a fantastic (and free!) resource packed with comprehensive information on all areas related to arts marketing and publicity.

This chapter focuses on marketing basics for the 'lone-ranger' co-op producer. First, a note about publicity. Although it is very much a part of the marketing drive, a lot of indie companies become confused when allocating tasks, so I will discuss it separately in the next chapter. In this book, 'marketing' refers to the ways you might sell your production directly to your *target audience* through advertising and promotional tools, whilst 'publicity' refers to how you might use *media relationships* to freely disseminate information and raise awareness of your show.

Let's imagine that your company is producing a 75 minute four-hander in a 100-seat venue. You have a total budget of about $13,000 with a projected income of approximately $16,000. The standard practice is to apportion 20% of your expected income to marketing expenses. This gives you $3000, most of which will be swallowed up by printing, newspaper directory and street press ads, so the more pro bono help you can find in areas such as design (postcards, invitations, website, e-flyers) and photography (preview and production shots), the more you can spend on other marketing initiatives. If you are working in a regional area, a smaller capital city or at a really tiny venue on a miniscule budget, you may only have a few hundred dollars to spend on marketing and publicity. To make the most of this enlist your friends' talents and maximise the use of low-cost tools such as free listings, email networks, show busking and your own walking boots for flyer distribution.

One of the biggest complaints from team members responsible for marketing shows is that they are not involved in the initial planning stages of a production. It helps if the artistic and marketing 'teams' are in sync right from the start, bouncing questions off each other like: where is the target audience for this production? Whether it's a commercial romp or a tough sell, it's better for everyone to understand what the gap between artistic product and audience response might be, and to implement strategy accordingly.

Working on little or no money for show promotion can be tough, but you can make it a more productive experience by following some simple rules. The following old-time phrases may seem a bit hackneyed now, but they embrace principles that really are worth their marketing weight in gold. Repeat after me:

1. My Brain Hurts!
2. It's All in the Timing
3. It's Who You Know
4. A Picture Paints a Thousand Words

1. My Brain Hurts!

Good. That means you're using your finest marketing asset. Too many small companies follow a well-trodden path of producing a flyer, distributing it and taking out a few street press ads, without thinking about *why* or *how* they are doing it. If you don't have much money, find ways of spreading the word that aren't used by everyone else. This is incredibly hard and you may only unearth one really great idea, but a single light bulb switched on at left field can transform a standard campaign into one that turns heads. Bribe as many colleagues as you can with alcohol or coffee and brainstorm. Look at your show from every angle and, most importantly, try to shift your thinking outside the square. If you decide to follow the time-honoured path of flyers, posters and ads, then use your collective brainpower to personalise the *how* of the exercise. How can you meld all your marketing tools into an efficient machine that stamps your company's personality on everything it releases? How do you entice a stranger to pick up your postcard above a zillion others? No wonder your brain hurts.

2. It's All in the Timing

Many small companies produce surprisingly good materials that simply don't hit the streets in time. The best design in the world will be an incredible waste of effort unless you have it in hand exactly when it's needed. A mistimed email campaign for discount tickets will end up everyone's junk-folders. Create a simple marketing schedule that regulates the flow of information and the execution of strategies and stick to it (see Schedule 8, page 106). When you have no money, timeliness is next to godliness.

3. It's Who You Know

It's no surprise that the line 'build it and they will come' is from a Hollywood movie. Who are 'they'? The unsuspecting public who will flock to your show just because it's on? Most independent shows rely heavily on the patronage of colleagues and friends to get them over the bottom line. Sure, you need to capture the imagination of the general public with scintillating copy and images, but in the meantime, your friends can get the ball rolling and word-of-mouth flowing. The same rule applies to finding sponsors and getting deals on printing, building materials and show consumables. Don't be frightened to exploit your social and business networks. A huge percentage of corporate partnerships (for both mainstream and independent companies) are sparked by a personal contact.

4. A Picture Paints a Thousand Words

Even if you have to starve for a week, or hock somebody's watch, pay a professional photographer to take decent photos, and make sure your graphic designer (whether paid or pro bono) is up to the task. Let me say that again: invest in fantastic images. This rule applies to postcard and poster images, publicity and production shots. Imagine the sort of mayhem you'd create waltzing down the main street of town wearing nothing but a red feather boa. An amazing image will get attention, even from people who don't give two hoots about theatre, and you won't get arrested either.

Basic tools

In that science fiction world of the unlimited budget, cashed-up companies create a plethora of printed items including glossy full-colour postcards, flyers, street and foyer posters, cigarette cards, promotional matchbooks and glow-in-the-dark keychains. In the gritty world of independent theatre, companies scrape together just enough money for a run of three thousand two-colour 120 gsm flyers. This is not as pitiful a comparison as it sounds. Aside from available cash flow, the difference in output can also be justified by scale; if you only have 100 seats to sell each night, then you really don't need the science-fiction print armoury.

Even without large amounts of cash you can turn the four principles above into a daily mantra, and apply liberally to all your promotion. One beautifully-designed, crisply-printed and well-distributed promotional tool (a flyer or postcard) can go a long way, and it's all that I'd recommend to groups on a cash-challenged budget.

Graphic design

Repeat mantra number four over and over. A beautifully-designed image or champion photo is worth gold. Many companies have friends or someone within the group who are talented enough to do a wonderful job, but if they are not able commit the time and effort required to get it looking just right, then bite the bullet and invest in paid, professional design. Buying stock images can be expensive, especially to use for multiple purposes (flyer, poster and website), but it can save you a lot of hassle. Check out a large online site like Getty's Images **[W25]** to see what's on offer.

How do you know what kind of image you are after? The inspiration for this may come out of your initial brain-hurting sessions, via discussions between the director, publicist and producer or perhaps there's a fun idea that's leapt out at everyone. The show, for example, is about internet dating and the postcard is laid-out like a 'profile' for one of the more quirky-looking cast members. Or perhaps you've decided to do a mixed run of postcards featuring several actors with witty photos and profiles. The image may be fun, moving or enigmatic, but at it *must* be *eye-catching, provocative, hilarious* or *aesthetically beautiful*. If you think a draft is 'nice' or 'pretty', 'expresses subtle themes', is 'neat and clear' or 'inoffensive', then scrap it and start again. Clarity is extremely important when it comes to copy, layout and general picture recognition, but you should be striving for maximum impact with your central image. I'm often surprised by talented groups who present engaging and colourful work and yet produce bland printed material. I suspect some companies try too hard to faithfully represent the themes and ideas of the play. Unfortunately, the subtleties of directorial vision don't always translate well into graphic design.

Let's say there is a company wishing to produce Sarah Kane's *Crave*. In initial discussions, the director, designer and producer knock around the themes and ideas and words and phrases like 'need and desire', 'abandonment', 'pain and isolation' and 'obsession' fill the conversation. They want to be true to the mood of the piece so they take a shadowy black and white photo of one of the actors, standing on a chair in a cell-like room. The photo has a moody, tragic feel to it. It's a high quality picture which the director feels perfectly captures the spirit of the production. But it's a terrible image for marketing purposes because the printed flyer telegraphs an atmosphere of doom and gloom to potential punters, even though there are hopeful, loving moments in this beautiful and moving play. The production turns out to be very good, but the image used to promote it gives audiences the impression that they are in for a tough night. The flyer, their only promotional tool, actually works against them.

Although it's important not to mislead potential punters, there is no rule that says your central image has to relate directly to an image or theme in your production. Sort through the ideas of the play, but if at the end of that discussion no words or pictures sing out, then perhaps you need to try another tack. Imagine if the *Crave* company had chosen to get out of the room and into a colourful field of flowers, and decided to go for an image of the same woman at a happier time, at the height of a passionate affair and in the throes of her 'craving'. Or if the image of 'craving' was suggested in a completely different way—by an old Mexican woman with no teeth eating a lush red apple, or a soldier running desperately for an about-to-be-missed train.

Think carefully about colour and what is needed to do full justice to your image. If you are depicting a lush environment or reproducing a colour photo, then spend the extra dollars on a sumptuous full-colour affair. On the other hand, many great flyers and posters have been created on a one or two-colour budget. A skilled designer should use light and shade to give a multi-dimensional overall feel. While many two-colour jobs include black as one of the colours, it's not compulsory—try experimenting with another colour for the text. Another option is to use one colour with a coloured paper stock for a two colour effect. (Heritage red or green on raw cardboard can give a lovely aged effect for example.) Black and white can be stunning, provided the image or photo has been drawn or shot with this in mind and the print quality is high. High gloss card looks fantastic, but dark hues attracts finger marks. The 'black, white and red' combination (two colours) is generally overused. In fact it's worth checking out several venues and cafes for printed material being distributed in the weeks and months before your show to get a feel for what's out there. If a particular design style or colour is over-represented, aim for contrast.

It is also possible to produce two images and print them together in the same run, so that you appear to have a couple of flyers on the market at the same time. This obviously makes more work for the designer, but should not cost much more to print. Many companies don't even consider this option, but it can really lift the look of a campaign, nabbing extra attention and making it look as though you've made a more significant investment. The main challenge with this will be to 'unite' the flyers so that it's obvious they're promoting the same show. Your aim is to increase impact, not reduce it.

Layout is as important (and individual) as your image. If you're doing it yourself with nifty software and not a lot of design experience, I've outlined a fairly foolproof format below.

Flyer/postcard front

Image, title of play and author, season dates, company name or logo, maybe a 'tag line'.

Keep the front as clean and striking as possible; have just enough information to grab attention and entice punters to turn it over. If you have a large image that fills the front, put the company name and logo on the back. If you are going for a mock format such as the 'dating profile' idea, tailor the essential information accordingly for maximum novelty impact. The use of a tag or 'strap' line can also be effective. This is a witty, poignant or strident one-liner that sums up the marketing thrust of the show, such as 'Just when you thought it was safe to go back to the nightclub ...' or 'The most controversial play of 2005'.

Flyer/postcard back

Title of play and author, company name/logo, dates, playing times and ticket prices, venue address, cast and design team, partner logos, booking details, 30–70 words about the play.

The back should contain all the essential information about the production (who, what, where, when, how much). Be careful not to crowd these critical snippets with rambling text about the play; fifty to seventy words is plenty. The text should be snappy and informative. Avoid esoteric and adjective-laden descriptions; punters want to know what the play is *about*, not your opinion of its artistic merits. If the play has won awards, throw that in. Quotes are also good, either for past productions by your company, or international productions of the play. If it's for a foreign production, make sure you credit the publication correctly (UK *Daily Telegraph*). Highlight any particularly strong selling points such as a controversial history or high-profile actors.

Once you've tossed around ideas and come up with a draft design, put yourself in the shoes of a punter. What does it suggest to you? Would you pick it up and turn it over to read details about the show? Would you put it in your pocket? Does it inspire you to find out more about the show or to think about booking? Give yourself plenty of time in the draft stage, so that you can show it to non-theatre friends and family who will give you honest feedback. If they don't respond very positively, then reconsider your approach.

Format

A popular printed configuration is the 'postcard flyer'. The clever 'postcards on a rack' set-up pioneered by Avante Card, engendered a promotional style in perfect synch with the funky interiors of inner-city cafes that blew every other format out of the water. As a practical tool they are perfect. Punters really do pick them up if they like the

wildcard productions & splinter theatre company
in association with b sharp present

BLAƆK MiJK

SEPTEMBER 23 TO OCTOBER 10

Set on a remote railway platform in a Russian hell-hole, Lyovchik and his heavily pregnant wife Poppet are two young Muscovites on the make. They have come to this rural backwater to flog faulty, overpriced Malaysian toasters to the peasantry. But when the train back to Moscow doesn't arrive, they find themselves trapped in the strange, cruel and whimsical world of provincial Russia.

Winner of the London Evening Standard Award for Most Promising New Playwright, Vassily Sigarev delivers a worm's eye view of post-Communist Russia as seen from the bottom of the heap.

BELVOIR ST DOWNSTAIRS THEATRE, 25 BELVOIR ST, SURRY HILLS

PERFORMANCE TIMES: TUES 7PM, WED - SAT 8.15PM, SUN 5.15PM
TICKET PRICES: ADULT $27, CONCESSION $21, GROUPS OF 5+ $23, PREVIEW $18 (WED 22 SEPT)
PAY WHAT YOU CHOOSE TUESDAYS: AVAILABLE 1 HOUR PRIOR TO PERFORMANCE. MINIMUM $10.

BOOKINGS (02) 9699 3444 OR **WWW.BELVOIR.COM.AU**

WRITTEN BY
Vassily Sigarev
TRANSLATED BY
Sasha Dugdale
DIRECTED BY
Sarah Goodes
WITH
Melanie Holt
Sam Haft
Sarah Woods
John Leary
Elaine Hudson
Jan Langford-Penny
Boris Brkic
Lenny Kovner
SET DESIGN
Genevieve Dugard
COSTUME DESIGN
Katrina Adams
LIGHTING DESIGN
Matt Cox
SOUND & MUSIC
Matteo Zingales
PRODUCED BY
Linden Goh
Peter Tehan

B SHARP

WILDCARDPRODUCTIONS.COM   SUPPORTING SPONSORS

Postcard design by Linden Goh. Photo (front) by Andy Baker, photo (back) by Craig O'Regan.

image, and use them for notes or even mail them as a real postcard. The indie scene leapt onto the idea and came up with more affordable ways to use and distribute them.

The best alternatives to the postcard are DL and A5 formats which are also very streamlined and easily distributed. Anything larger isn't as easy to pick up and pocket, and tends to look messy on shelves and ledges. Postcards and DL flyers are best for mailing since they fit nicely into a DL envelope without folding.

The past few years have seen the demise in popularity of the cafe poster. Whilst they are still a viable tool in smaller communities, in capital cities (particularly Sydney) establishments are less inclined to cover up their trendily painted feature walls. They are also very expensive to distribute professionally. Nevertheless, posters can be very attractive and are great for archival records, venue display, to frame as gifts for sponsors and supporters, or as raffle prizes. The advance of the digital age means you can produce single high-quality poster-sized colour outputs. If your cast and crew frequent several coffee shops, then it may be worth getting 30 or so digitally printed so they can personally distribute them to these places.

Street posters, however, which are expensive to produce and distribute are generally beyond the means of indie companies. Don't even think about doing it yourself. Pole-wrapping and bill-postering is an illegal activity 'controlled' by companies who won't take kindly if you stomp on their turf. As a DIY exercise, it's shady work that's best avoided.

Printed tools which are generally under used are the 'cigarette card' and the 'bookmark'. They are neither suitable nor warranted for every production, but if you want to promote your show in partnership with commercial groups such as hairdressers, cab drivers, bookstores or restaurants, it's very convenient for supporters to tuck them in a bill or with a purchased book or hand out with change or a receipt. You might also think of printing something on the back that encourages customers to pop them in their wallets, such as a calendar or handy transport information.

Printing

When you compare printing charges, you'll discover that the range of quotes for a single item such as the simple postcard will be as wide as it is perplexing. Never was the adage 'you get what you pay for' more applicable. There are plenty of el cheapo offset printing companies that will print large quantities at competitive rates, but may also burden you with poor quality image reproduction and trimming, inaccurate colour, and worst of all, late delivery. It's really important that all these elements are taken into consideration when choosing a printer, as a great saving dollar-wise will never make up for the loss of impact rendered by a sloppy and unattractive print job that's late to boot. Start with quality and then work on price. You can collect great flyers and postcards and trace their origins, but the best recommendations will be from other small companies who've found printing outfits they can rely on. Good printers give great advice and can even help you to save money. Quiz colleagues about their experiences and don't be afraid to ask for samples of the printer's work.

If you want decent coverage, you'll need about 3000 flyers, but if you are getting them professionally distributed, consider printing 5000–10,000. Printing costs work on an economy of scale; the more you print, the smaller the cost gap gets. Calculate every potential use for the flyers such as general and personal distribution, direct mailing, invitations, media kits and show venue top-ups. If this adds up to more than 5000, then print 10,000 and increase your distribution coverage.

When planning your print jobs consider the following:

- Decide the format and details of your job (DL or other, single or double-sided, paper type and weight, colours and quantity) *before* starting the quote process so that you can compare quotes accurately.

- Check out different paper stocks. GSM (grams per square metre) refers to weight. It may be tempting to go for a lower GSM to save money, but if you are producing a postcard, it will seem odd if it has the thickness and weight of a loose leaf page. By the same token, the money you save on less expensive paper stock can be used to upgrade your flyer from one colour to two.

- Do a triple detail check (two company members and someone outside the process with a 'fresh eye') of all show details and spelling, particularly of names. Artists and crew may happily work on a co-op basis, but will be understandably furious if their names are inaccurately spelled on a widely-circulating promotional tool.

- You are much more likely to get what you want if you ask lots of questions, so don't just hand your artwork over and hope for the best. Good printers are very knowledgeable, love a challenge and may help you find a more economical way of printing (they might suggest a slightly different paper size which will fit more on a sheet for example).

- Always see a printer's proof. Make sure that there is a proper sign-off procedure in place, so that nothing is printed until any corrections have been made and you've given the go ahead

- If you're going for budget printing, you're more likely to end up with the colours you've selected if you do a one or two colour job rather than a full colour one. Full colour is actually a mix of four colours (Cyan, Magenta, Yellow and Black); a slight variation in the mix of these can produce inaccurate results. One and two colour jobs use pre-mixed inks, which can be more accurately matched to a Pantone colour chart.

- Consider sharing print runs with other companies. Some printers specialise in certain formats (such as DL for galleries) or small runs and often print a number of jobs together. Bear in mind though that you won't have so much control over timing or quality.
- Investigate the possibilities of developing a partnership with a printer that may attract discounts in exchange for contra advertising in programs and other promotional material. It's quite difficult these days to secure paper sponsors, but it's worth a try.
- Save money by sticking to the same format for launch or fundraising flyers, show flyers and opening night invitations, and printing them together.

Distribution

If you have a large team, a very tight budget or are targeting a mostly local audience, then it's entirely possible for the team to distribute promotional material by hand. If this is your preferred method, co-ordinate the process so that hotspots are covered and doubling up which wastes precious flyers avoided.

Plan a distribution campaign using street directory maps and identifying key hotspots such as libraries, cafes, bookshops and venues. It's a bit of a cheat, but you can save time on research by checking out the websites of professional distribution companies that list major public outlets. Match small areas to company members according to lived-in or convenient suburbs and give everyone a deadline for distribution. It shouldn't be hard for each member to spend one afternoon placing a handful of flyers in 10–20 strategic locations in their neighbourhood. If you can garner enough enthusiasm and you have a good quantity of flyers, then plan a second assault mid-way through the run. Make a list of 10 places that should be checked regularly (including your show venue!) and make each member responsible for topping up flyers in a couple of outlets.

Professional distribution saves a lot of time and, in capital cities where you need widespread coverage, it's almost essential. The standard of services definitely varies though. Seek advice from season-based companies, venues or galleries who use such services regularly; if a distribution company is still doing a thorough and timely job for them after a year, then you can be pretty sure it's reliable.

Good distributors will have lists of areas and locations they service, so that you can choose an inner-city or typical 'arts' run or add in suburbs that you feel appropriate. Flyer distribution costs average around $100 per thousand. Some companies will charge according to the number of outlets you choose rather than quantity.

It is possible to get costs down considerably by guaranteeing distributors multiple runs through the year. Many curated seasons save lots of money this way, so think about banding together with other indie companies who have shows planned throughout the year and cut a deal.

If you have a show with a particular target audience (Chinese, gay and lesbian, office workers), you could use a professional service for general arts coverage, and split 'specialised' suburbs amongst members of the team.

Direct mail

Just a brief word on this, since 99% of indie companies don't have the resources to collect, track and analyse the kind of audience data which forms the basis of direct mail campaigns. Sophisticated box-office systems can record many details about each patron who books, allowing venues and companies to build a profile of their audience members and how often they attend. You may not be able to get enough data to know the age/gender/buying profile of your audience, but you should at least be able to capture some basic contact details.

Collecting patron data on the indie scene isn't as hard as it sounds, but it may take quite a while especially if you don't have your own box-office system. You could start by setting up a guest book for all performances in a prominent position in the foyer, allowing patrons to fill in their details if they want to receive information about future shows. Offer an incentive, such as the opportunity to go into a draw for a (sponsored!) dinner for two at a local restaurant or free tickets to another show. You may only have a couple of hundred names after a year of productions, but they will be people who want to hear from you, and you can develop a relationship.

Record the data into Excel spreadsheets, which can be 'sorted' according to your needs during various promotional exercises. They can also be used for 'mail merging', a simple Microsoft Word function that allows you to create and 'personalise' letters effortlessly and create mailing labels. Follow the Help section in Word or Excel or visit Microsoft's online site **[W20]** for tutorial assistance.

The revised Privacy Amendment Act of 2000 (as it pertains to private-sector business) is based on 10 National Privacy Principles **[W30]** which relate to the collection, storage and use of an individual's personal information. This means that you can only use contact details for the 'primary purpose of collection'. You cannot use mail and email addresses for marketing purpose unless they have been given to you for that purpose and it's no longer possible for companies to pass on the private details of any individual to a third party.

This means that even though your company may be using the box-office system of a venue or may be part of a curated season, you may not have direct access to the information about people who attend your show, or carte blanche use of it. It's worth chatting with someone in the marketing department about the venue's privacy policy, and appropriate distribution and use of ticket buyer information. The days of buying, selling and exchanging lists are over. Small companies must find other ways of capturing contact details for people interested in their work, so they can develop loyal audience members.

Most small companies use email to reach 'customers' they think they might have a relationship with, and in doing so can underestimate the more direct power of a catchy pitch in hard copy. In the age of computer viruses, 'attachment-opening' fear and relentless spamming, a well-written letter with a genuine offer has weight and can seem positively genteel. And *personal*, which is the point of the exercise.

Direct mail is a *communication* tool, so don't just cram envelopes with promotional material. Include a letter (personalised, if the size of the list is manageable) which:

- Refers to the relationship (ie 'as a previous attendee of our shows, we would like to …)
- Offers some brief information about the show or your company that *isn't* on the enclosed flyer
- Includes a buying incentive, such as an special deal for preview or the first week of performances
- Is signed by a key member of the company, or someone with a public profile who is part of the show or affiliated with the company

Email marketing

Email campaigns have become a standard feature of marketing for shows at every venue level, as it is cheap and promises swift and direct delivery. It's a medium that's generally poorly used by the sector, though, and a lot of information gets summarily junked by frustrated recipients before it is read. Privacy laws also apply to email marketing. When you collect patron addresses, the person needs to agree to their use in marketing expressly. Indie companies mostly use email marketing to spread the word amongst colleagues, family and friends, and whilst it's unlikely that persons known to the company will object to receiving promotional emails, you should make sure that there are clear contact details on each email, that enable the recipient to 'unsubscribe'.

Email promotions can work wonders when material is cleverly designed, includes interesting information or a genuine ticket deal, and doesn't land in the same inbox five times in the one day. If the company has built up a patron email list (non-industry), then the producer or company member responsible for marketing should manage this list and be the sole initiator of emails to it. The biggest emailing mistakes made by small companies relate to frequency of contact, file size and repetitive information that offers no incentive to buy tickets. If the whole company decides to email their personal contact lists ad-hoc, then you'll end up with a spamming effect that will just annoy the hell out of everyone you know.

When spruiking your show via email, consider the following:

- **Planning and timing:** A simple strategy that doesn't clog the airwaves is to choose three or four specific dates for controlled email releases; six weeks and two weeks before opening night, and again during the first week. If houses are slow, add one more date in the final week.

- **Frequency:** Although it's hard to avoid cross-over contact in the indie sector, you should try and find ways to prevent email bombardment. If five actors have pretty similar email contact lists, then perhaps let everyone have free rein on the first email release date but split the other dates amongst company members. Demand abstinence at all other times, except for fresh contacts! A recipient getting an email every couple of days will only get annoyed.

- **Targets:** Aside from encouraging friends and colleagues to attend, email marketing is a great way to promote to specific groups and 'opinion leaders' such as hairdressers, butchers, teachers, youth groups; whoever your ideal targets are.

- **Variety:** E-flyers are a great invention, and a cheap investment with potentially very good returns. The trouble is, if the same e-flyer circulates for a couple of months it soon becomes too-easily junked. If someone in your group has the software and skills to create a range of alternative e-flyers, then tie them to the computer and demand output! Wildcard Productions, one of the 2004 B Sharp companies, created a series of teaser flyers using some great images from a publicity photo shoot. Whenever a recipient opened mail from them, they received a different image with a funny caption; the campaign remained quirky and fresh throughout the season. If you don't have a web-whiz at your disposal, then at least make sure that the emails you send out on your release dates are *different* in some way, possibly adding a new layer of information about the show, or a news update such as a review or other public feedback. Personalise whenever possible.

    This practice can be extended into a soft form of 'viral marketing', where a joke, doctored image or funny video clip is used in conjunction with product information, to encourage recipients to pass the email on. Cook up something really inspiring with your web-whiz and take your e-marketing to the next level!

- **Size:** Under no circumstances should you send large attachments or files that clog or crash recipients' computers. Any image 500 kb or over is going to cause inconvenience (and a lot of cursing) somewhere out there in cyberspace.

- **Privacy:** Make sure that the email includes contact details for the company, and a brief sentence at the bottom of your email giving recipients a chance to 'opt out' from further contact. Always use the 'bcc' (blind carbon copy) function when sending group emails. Do this by sending the message *to* yourself and then *bcc* it to everyone else. This protects the identity of individuals on your email lists. Neglecting to bcc is a terrible invasion of privacy.

- **Hygiene:** Ensure that everyone who is sending out emails (particularly if attachments are involved) uses anti-virus software to prevent the spread of nasties. Keep your lists up-to-date, and monitor bounce-backs carefully. If someone notifies you of a change of address (or a preferred address for marketing contact), then deal with it immediately.

Make sure that offers are distributed carefully; direct mail recipients won't be impressed if they book on the basis of a mail offer, only to find a better deal land in their inbox through a competing discount. Stick to one or two types of offers and 'brand' them (eg: the 'early bird two-for-one special'), so that box office staff can easily identify genuine targets.

Many indie companies are building websites, which include everything from information about past, current and future shows, to interviews with company members, sound and video bites and downloadable publicity shots. If you have a website, make sure your URL is included on all promotional material, and that the website has additional information to that generally circulating, to make it worth the browse. Frequent updates (reviews and audience feedback), plus postings of special web offers encourage repeat visits. If you are part of a season hub or working in an established venue, then request a link from their website to yours. Make sure you provide a direct link from your website to the season hub's online booking service.

E-newsletters are also a great way of staying in touch with patrons and colleagues during non-production periods. Consider developing a monthly or bi-monthly e-letter that includes fresh information about the company and perhaps updates on other indie shows. Enhance your own newsletter with offers from other companies and sponsor or local businesses.

Advertising

Advertising in the major dailies is too expensive for most small companies, though sometimes 'distress' space (unsold advertising space) becomes available at very short notice and is offered at substantial discounts. You may not advertise enough to build the kind of relationship to be offered this, but perhaps your venue does, especially if you are working in a curated season. Ask them to let you know if any distress space is offered at a time that might work for your production. You may nab a really good deal.

In Sydney it's very hard to avoid the *Sydney Morning Herald* Theatre Directory, the major daily theatre listing for the city, for the run of your show. A basic listing which includes the title, playwright, company, venue and dates will cost between $300 and $400 per week. There are similar listings available in other cities, but they don't have the same 'must do' force.

You may find it helpful to build a relationship with the street press ('alternative' and arts-specific weekly and monthly newspapers). If you have a show that's particularly targeted at the young funky adult or alternative scene, consider taking out a series of ads, which will put you in a good position to negotiate a discount. On average, a '10 x 2' ad will cost you between $200 and $270 dollars in a street press rag. Despite the protestations of some editors to the contrary, buying advertising will almost certainly garner you a chunk of editorial. Street press can be generous with small companies particularly if the arts editor is interested in a company or show, which could result in some sponsored advertising. You may get ads cheaper or free, or in-house graphic design paid for, for instance. When you are talking to the advertising manager of a street rag, make sure you ask about the options. Community radio is a very underrated marketing medium for indie companies and for a relatively small amount of money, you can get pretty decent advertising coverage. You may be able to negotiate a deal, for example, where the station covers the cost of ad production, whilst the company pays for airtime.

All reputable media marketing outlets have kits that include costs and detailed consumer statistics; collect these and study them before purchasing advertising. Even a cheap deal will be a waste of money if a particular publication or radio program isn't going to reach the right demographic.

Odd and ends

Unless you think the impact will be stunning, it's not really worth spending too many dollars on gimmicks. If you are working in a regional area where everyone will wear your hats and T-shirts, it might help brand awareness, and if you can get it sponsored then you've nothing to lose. I've received fancy key-rings, matches and magnets from indie companies that I know are strapped for cash, but rather than impressing me with their cleverness, I've always worried about what will be missing from their next production. There may come a time when promotional merchandise will be worth considering, but perhaps not in your first few years of working as a co-operative.

One of the most arresting forms of free marketing I've seen is 'chalking'. In most states any kind of marketing on public property is illegal, but I've seen some clever and beautiful work wrought on pavements, that isn't permanent or harmful to anyone. If you work in a local community or suburb, perhaps you could negotiate permission with local businesses to do some wall chalking? Design it to be aesthetically pleasing (employ a professional pavement 'artist') and remove it thoroughly when the show is over.

Some other marketing opportunities to consider are cinema-slide advertising (think independent arthouse cinemas), placing ads in theatre programs for other productions, local newsletters and newspapers and street-busking, which is easier for shows that have a comic, visual or musical element.

You might also consider bartering a mutually 'active' exchange of flyers at venues. Some venues won't allow 'seat-drops' because they are messy and visually distracting in small theatres, but will organise for Front of House staff to hand flyers to patrons. If you distribute flyers outside any establishment (including your performance venue), make sure you get permission first from the venue management.

Marketing your show strongly and imaginatively is hard work, but the rewards can be very satisfying. If one or more collaborators can brainstorm effectively, create realistic timelines and carry out tasks efficiently, there is no reason why your company can't create a first class in-house marketing campaign.

SCHEDULE 8: Sample Marketing Schedule (pre-production)

Week 7
- Planning
- Finalise marketing budget
- Draft media release
- Finalise flyer artwork

Week 6
- Promotional photo shoot
- Design e-flyers
- Finalise media release

Week 5
- Distribute media release
- Draft direct mail letter
- Release e-flyer #1: Teaser

Week 4
- Print and distribute flyers
- Finalise direct mail letter

Week 3
- Design street press ad
- Post direct mail-out

Week 2
- Run street press ad #1
- Release e-flyer #2: Ticket offer
- Re-distribute media release

Week 1
- Run street press ad #2
- Book theatre listing

Production week
- Run street press ad #3
- Release e-flyer #3
- Run theatre listing #1

⑥

Getting the lead

Plugged-in publicity

One of the major decisions a company makes when planning a show is whether to employ a professional publicist, or to engage in a do-it-yourself blitz. If you are working in a season hub situation you may be provided with publicity support, but most companies will need to find their own way to get the message out there via the media monolith. A company's choice will depend almost entirely on budget, the level of communication skills within the company and access to media lists and contacts.

The fee for a professional publicist will certainly swallow a big chunk of your budget and well may you ask, is it worth it? Firstly, consider the balance you are able to strike between marketing and publicity; if you have little or no money to spend on advertising, then you will need to rely much more heavily on publicity.

If you are a fairly new company without internal publicity experience, working in a premium small venue, then it's probably worth hiring a publicist. You'll be competing in a tough market and you're already making a sizeable investment in venue and marketing costs, so you don't want to bungle it on the publicity front. If your season is running in a small community, for a targeted audience or for a few low-key performances, it can probably be managed within the group. The same could apply if you've done a few shows and your producer is media savvy and has developed lists and contacts. A lot of companies will try to save money in this area if their costs are already high, yet to recoup those costs you need bums on seats. If you really don't have the internal resources to manage publicity well, then it makes sense to employ a publicist to help boost your chances of improving the bottom line.

The Hired Gun

There are big publicity firms with offices in every state, small companies with just a few employees, and individuals with corporate experience who offer themselves as solo guns for hire. Prices vary. I've seen fees for small shows range from $1500 to $3500 in capital cities, depending on the profile of the publicity company, their interest in the job (profile of creatives) and the likelihood that it may lead to further work (for example, if the show is part of a season hub).

The first thing you need to know is that it's perfectly acceptable to negotiate fees (average for a capital city production is between $2000–$2500 exclusive of consumables, anything under this is a bargain). Your success will depend on the factors above and how much work the publicist already has on their plate; you may have better luck at the beginning or end of a traditionally busy show period. It's a big financial outlay, so do some research and compare quality and price. There may be three or four publicists (or less) to choose from in your city, so make the time to meet them and ask for quotes. Reputable publicists will have written information that clearly outlines exactly what you get for your dough and they should also advise about additional costs. A publicist's fee will rarely cover consumables such as paper for invites, photo reproduction and media kits, mailing and faxing costs and couriers; if they estimate more than $500 for this, then ask for a breakdown of projected costs. Compare quotes and job breakdowns thoroughly and do some bartering. If it's a quiet time on the scene and more than one publicist is hungry for work, you may be able to get fees down a bit. The following gives you a rough idea of what you can expect to get for a $2000–3000 fee. The publicist would normally:

- Meet with core collaborators and discuss angles (actors, director, writers or current events)
- Read the play and attend a run of the show toward the end of the rehearsal period
- Provide a written publicity plan (of who will be approached and when)
- Chase arts preview stories/interviews for mainstream street and local press
- Organise 'free listings'
- Set up radio interviews (and TV if appropriate)
- Accompany artists to major interviews (commercial radio, TV)
- Write a media release and distribute it
- Create opening night invitations using letterhead (unless invitations are specially printed), mail them and take RSVPs
- Chase reviewers and distribute photos
- Create media packs for opening night
- Attend opening night and liaise with media
- Provide a 'WIP' (work-in-progress update) to the producer each week
- Follow-up any post-opening media interest
- Provide a publicity report (including media cuttings) within a few weeks of the show closing

You've done your research and collected quotes and now it's time to choose. Should you automatically go for the cheapest deal? If your budget is particularly tight there may be no other option, but first assess the track record of the publicist on the indie scene. Have they worked in other small venues? What sort of coverage do they generally aim for (don't be afraid to ask!)? If you have the money, it may be tempting to go for a bigger company with a number of in-house publicists, but remember such outfits will be handling a lot of high profile clients simultaneously and may not give priority to a small job. And though they may have great contacts in the mainstream media, if your project is hard to pitch to this sector, you may be better off with a solo publicist who pitches small projects day-in and day-out and knows the street press and the alternative media. Be wary of publicists who have only worked in related industries such as film. Theatre protocol, practices and journos are very specific and you want to be sure that your publicist has the industry nous and contacts that you are paying for. They may have worked on major films and have fabulous credits, but if they don't have the right media lists, can't organise your free listings and don't know the reviewers, then their experience will be of little use.

Another thing to consider when you are selecting a publicist is their level of *interest.* I believe it's important that the person or company who is publicising your show demonstrates a genuine interest in indie work: they don't have to love your particular play (or production) to do their job well, but an interest in 'the alternative' is helpful. If they're used to handling mainstream shows or musicals featuring big names, they will know that pitching for an indie show full of fresh faces takes a lot more time and effort. The most impressive publicists I have worked with have demonstrated loyalty to their poorer and more 'underground' clients by showing an active interest and pushing just that little bit harder for them. If a publicist asks to read the script and chat with you properly about the production before taking it on, it's a good sign that they choose to work with productions that they are interested in and feel confident they can promote.

So, what sort of 'success' can you expect from this person or company you've given a big chunk of hard-earned cash to? There are many fantastic publicists out there who will work hard for indie shows, but publicity is not an exact science. The amount of media attention they can attract for your production will depend on a number of factors. You can make suggestions to a publicist and ask them to seek coverage from particular publications, columns or journalists, but you need to be realistic. The media is only interested in interviewing artists and running stories on productions which they believe will interest their readers or audience. If your production and personnel doesn't grab them, your publicist is unlikely to be able to convince them otherwise. That doesn't mean the publicist shouldn't push as many angles as they can in the hope of getting bites, and if they take your money and *then* tell you not to expect anything but a bit of local or street press, then you have a genuine right to complain. As your company gains more experience with publicity you'll be better able to tell when coverage is thin because the publicist isn't active enough or because the show (or angles being pitched) doesn't grab the media at the time.

Despite some wonderful arts journalists and editors who are as passionate about theatre as artists themselves, on the whole, the media is a fairly shallow beast. There's no shame in learning what it likes to eat and feeding it accordingly! Most publicity is good publicity, and many good productions have failed with the belief that the 'worthiness' of the coverage needs to match the artistic weight of the show. Don't be frightened to play up angles that are tasty to the beast, even if it isn't what you'd choose to consume yourself.

So, how do you get the most out of your hired gun? Do you need to tail them constantly, checking that they have their firing chambers loaded and ready for action? There's a big difference between maintaining regular contact with a publicist and hassling them to death. If you phone daily with demands for mainstream stories and by-the-minute updates your voicemails will lose force. The majority of professional publicists have a number of jobs on the go at once, and very competently negotiate difficult editorial territory with limited opportunities. The relationship you have with your publicist is an invaluable one. You will get the best out of it if you:

● Do a bit of research so that you have a general understanding of media opportunities in your city or region. Brainstorm angles with your team *before* meeting with your publicist. Don't be frightened to share your ideas, but let them go if they are not practical. The more enthusiastic and well-informed your company is, the more fuel your publicist will have to stoke the fire. If you have specific or special media contacts, let the publicist know. If the media contact is a very personal one (or culturally/socially specific), and you choose to make an approach yourself make sure this is clearly understood by all parties. You can make the initial approach and the publicist follows up, or perhaps the publicist handles all general theatrical media and the company pitches the show to the ethnically-specific media it has close contacts with.

● Have a transparent discussion with your publicist at the outset about what sort of publicity is achievable, what coverage might be possible with some pushing, and what they consider to be a long shot or totally unrealistic. If you have expectations about certain media sectors or publications, then discuss this up-front. Be aware of any sectors (culturally or socially specific) that won't be covered by a mainstream publicist. Ask for a written publicity plan, or take notes of this meeting so that you can monitor progress rationally and realistically. If you feel things are going terribly awry, you can use the plan or notes as a point of reference.

● Nominate *one* company member (preferably the producer or stage manager—someone in close and constant contact with the creatives) to liaise with your publicist. Ideally, the publicist will regularly send updated publicity schedules (a Work in Progress or

WIP) to show how pitches are progressing, as well as ensuring that the stage manager and creatives are aware of upcoming interviews. If they are doing their job and keeping you in the loop, you shouldn't have to contact them too often for general updates. Try to save your enquiries for specific questions or to share ideas or fresh contacts. An uninspiring 'How's it going?', will probably be met with an equally non-committal answer. If you feel your publicist is dragging their heels, then quiz them about specific publications or interviews that they have been chasing.

- Publicists will not automatically attend all interviews. If the interviewees are confident and experienced, the publicist probably won't, unless it's to make an introduction. If an actor or director is nervous or inexperienced, if there is a sensitive issue that needs stepping around (the actor has just got out of rehab for example), or if it's a major interview, then ask your publicist to attend.

- Your publicist may be the shiny gun, but only you can provide the bullets. The quicker you get the following together, the quicker your publicist can start working for you effectively. Arm your publicist with *written* information about the show for the press release, brief biographies of cast and crew (*not* lengthy CVs, but one or two paragraphs for each person), a contact list including mobile phone numbers for actors and most importantly, some good publicity or rehearsal shots in digital form. More on this vital 'armoury' a bit later.

It's important also to brief the hired gun on your publicity 'history'; have there been recent articles or major press profiles on the company or creatives that may influence coverage for this show? If you know a journalist has a particular interest in an actor or director, then let the publicist know.

So, when should you jump up and down and complain? If your publicist is rude or evasive, sends out press releases or invitations late, is impossible to contact, doesn't update you from week to week, or hasn't chased up contacts that you have given them within a reasonable timeframe, then get pushy. If you are halfway through your campaign and the planned publicity cocktail has been neither shaken nor stirred, organise a meeting, armed with your plan/notes and some reasonable demands for greater attention to the task at hand.

The DIY cowboys and cowgirls

Many indie companies have a producer or a core group of collaborators who can promote their small-scale shows as well as highly-paid publicists. The most successful are companies with good communicators who *enjoy* liaising with journalists, editors and presenters on the phone and in theatre foyers. Over a couple of years, such companies will build up media and invitation lists and contacts. If there is no single designated producer, then for each production there will be a dedicated publicity contact who is *not* part of the current artistic ensemble. He or she will work outside the rehearsal room, sending out information, pitching for stories and reviews and taking RSVPs.

So, does your company have what it takes to mount a self-propelled publicity drive? Ask yourselves: have you collated or do you have access to all relevant contacts for local, street and mainstream media? Is there someone in the group who is friendly, engaging, efficient and patient and who has good written and verbal communication skills? Do they have a mobile phone that can remain switched on during the day as well as a decent computer and reliable email address? Can they respond quickly to replies and requests from the media? Will they be able to dedicate themselves to publicity tasks in the busy seven to ten days prior to opening night? If you answered yes to all these questions, then maybe it's time to take on the challenge for yourselves. If it's an effort to talk someone in the group into it, or if everyone is in rehearsal for the show or has a day job that keeps them away from a phone and computer for most of the day, then reconsider raising funds for a hired gun.

Building media lists and contacts

At the very least, you will need a list of contacts for all major theatre media (newspapers, magazines, radio and internet) including theatre

Ewen Leslie in the Tamarama Rock Surfers production of *Cross Sections*. Photo: John Buckley

reviewers, as well as street press and local newspapers. You will also need to be aware of the 'free-listings' opportunities in your area.

Many indie companies compile lists and contacts over time via fairly ad-hoc methods. Lists are lent and borrowed by affiliated companies, 'pinched' from publicists and supplemented by hard-slog methods such as reading and researching newspapers and magazines and making direct calls to media organisations for current contacts. The internet has made it much easier for companies to research media outlets and gain direct access to many journalists via email for major, street and local theatre media. But there is a mountain of smaller non-theatre outlets and opportunities waiting in the misty land of 'other media'. Publicity companies who build up extensive, diverse and often very personal media lists and contacts are extremely protective of their booty and for very good reason. It takes time to create and maintain them, and to forge relations with particular contacts. If you are starting from scratch, try investing in a media guide, which is a comprehensive compilation of Australian media outlets. There are a number of online versions which are regularly updated. Check out Media Monitors **[W31]**, AAP **[W32]** and the Margaret Gee Media Guide **[W33]**. Guides are pretty expensive for struggling indie companies, but a worthy investment if you intend to mount several shows in a year.

Tools of the Trade

Whatever option you choose, you'll need to develop three basic tools for each show, which will enable you or your publicist to start firing at media targets.

The Media Release

This vital document is the key to disseminating information about your show to the big wide world. It's the primary bait for media nibbles and bites and may be quoted verbatim in some articles, so make sure you spend quality time writing, reviewing and re-writing. Ensure that the final result is clear and juicy, with all the tastiest bits on display for easy consumption. There's a multitude of ways to present information in a media release. Here's a simple formula:

- Keep it strictly to one A4 page between 500 and 600 words. Additional pages only encourage you to ramble—it's also easy to lose half of a two-page release on someone's busy, paper-filled desk.

- Clearly brand the page 'Media Release' and place key information at the top; the Who, What, When and Where (Flying Pigs Productions presents 'Ham and Away' by Cheryl Bacon at the Ambassador Theatre from 1–31 July). The reader should be able to register major details instantly.

  Follow with a couple of juicy lines (no more than three) in bold. This could be a striking media quote from a previous show ('The Flying Pigs will make your feet stomp and your heart soar ...'), a media quote from an international production of the play or some witty lines from the play itself.

- Create a leading paragraph for the body of your release, that exposes something catchy or saleable about the show. This could be about an actor (Marion Taylor, winner of this years AFI Award for Best Actress for her stunning performance in *The Flowers are Blue* makes her Melbourne stage debut in...), the company (Following last year's cult-hit production of *Love in Warsaw*, Battleground Productions present...) or something controversial about the play (On its opening night in Paris in December 1886 Alfred Jarry's *Ubu Roi* caused a riot of previously unknown proportions...)

- The body of your release is the 'meat' of the story; a lively outline of plot, themes and issues and more about your creative team. Actors' names should be followed by their most interesting credits in brackets.

- The release may be used for articles, reviews, interviews, listings and announcements, so follow the body with *full* season details; specific show times, ticket prices and methods of booking.

- Conclude your release with your contact details in bold and separated from the body of text for easy reference: a name, phone number and email address for enquiries and further information.

- Check carefully for spelling mistakes or errors in information, paying particular attention to names and show dates and times.

- Layout: If you are faxing or mailing, use standard white A4 paper, and avoid fancy graphics and fonts. 11 point Arial Black for regular paragraphs and up to 18 point for headings is easy to read. Avoid huge slabs of text by breaking sections into more easily digestible paragraphs. Don't overuse bold or italics. Save these formats for information you need to stand out such as titles and names. Create distinction by adding the logo of your company and, if necessary, those of your sponsors. Fancy logos can dramatically increase the size of a standard word document; be careful of exceeding the 1mb mark.

Remember that your release is a practical tool for media who are looking for solid information for their readers; the writing-style is very different to that used for producing brochure copy. A release isn't a direct sales pitch to patrons, it's meant to engage the interest of media professionals to encourage them to interview creatives and write stories for their readers/viewers. Sweeping, evocative and adjective-laden descriptions are fine for a couple of sentences, so long as there is a genuine core of grounded information following the hype. If a journalist gets to the end of the release and isn't clear on what the show is about, or can't find critical information such as times, dates and contacts (think What, When, Who, Why?), then it's more likely to be discarded. As you get more experienced creating releases, experiment with your writing style, layout and design, but first-timers should keep it clear, engaging and simple. Check out releases on professional theatre company websites if you need some guidance.

A cut-down version for free listings (brief mentions in theatre and entertainment guides that don't cost anything) is also advisable; include all critical information and contacts and an interesting, to-the-point paragraph describing the show.

Finally, when you are emailing your release, cut and paste it into the body of the email as well as attaching it, in case the recipient experiences difficulties when trying to open it.

Biographies

In addition to your media release, the producer should ask all creatives and crew to prepare a two-paragraph biography of career highlights *before* rehearsals commence. Full-length CVs are cumbersome for busy publicists who don't have time to pick through dozens of credits for ads and indie shows. I have experienced huge resistance from

The Working Group

B SHARP

The Working Group in association with B Sharp presents

FAUSTUS

Previews 16 March. Season March 17– April 10 2005

Written by **Robert Couch after Christopher Marlowe**

Directed by **Joe Couch**

With **Paul Ashton, Eden Falk, Amie McKenna, Rebecca Smee** & **Jo Turner**

"Hell is where we are."

Meet John Faustus: 22 years old, genius, read every book in the world. But John's feeling rather restless, and when the candlelight burns past midnight, his gaze turns to the underworld.

Meet Mephistophilis: ageless, provocateur, assistant to Satan. Mephistophilis is finding the soul trade a repetitive game, especially these days when it's a buyer's market (a bit like real estate). But when she meets John Faustus, the bargain struck is a little unusual. Mephistophilis will get John's soul, as is standard, but John not only gets 24 years of power, he also gets Mephistophilis as his servant. Therein begins a titanic clash of two opposites. Impetuous and passionate, John Faustus shatters every barrier his wily demon can create. Defiant to the end, he fights for existence itself.

This re-writing of **Faustus** is a father/son collaboration between Robert and Joe Couch. Robert's previous plays include *When Voyaging* (1975) and *Batavia* (National Playwrights' Conference 1995). Joe has just completed the inaugural Richard Wherret Fellowship at Sydney Theatre Company. Previous directing credits include *The Cosmonaut's Last Message to the Woman He Once Loved in the Former Soviet Union* (Company B 2002), and *Away* (STC 2004). The Couch adaptation of Marlowe's play is extensive. Says Joe "There's probably less than 50 lines of the original, and really only a handful of scenes remain indebted to Marlowe. We've abandoned the dated theology of the original, keeping the play's spirit to create an incisive critique of the world's current religious wars."

This raw and punchy telling of a man and his pact with the devil is delivered by The Working Group, who created the sell-out sensation **Knives in Hens** (B Sharp 2002). **Faustus** is the opening production in the B Sharp 2005 Season, a unique partnership between Company B and independent theatre companies, now in its seventh year. The 2005 B Sharp Season will be launched on Monday 28 February 2005.

Production Team: Sound Design **Stephan Gregory** Lighting Design **Damien Cooper**
Set Design **Steven Butler** Costume Design **Ailsa Paterson** Producer **Kate Armstrong-Smith**
Production Manager **Claire Portek**

Faustus
Belvoir St Downstairs Theatre, 25 Belvoir Street, Surry Hills
Previews: Wednesday 16 March. Season: Thursday 17 March – Sunday 10 April
Times: Tuesday 7.00pm. Wednesday–Saturday 8.15pm. Sunday 5.15pm.
Adult: $27 Concession: $21 Groups: $23 Preview: $18
Cheap Tuesday: Pay what you can. $10 minimum.
Bookings: 02 9699 3444 / www.belvoir.com.au

Media enquiries contact:
Publicist, Company: Phone details, email details

Media release prepared by Sarah Wilson for Mollison Communications actors to writing about themselves, but collecting biographies at the start of the process saves a lot of pain and wasted time further down the track. Assure them that dot-point highlights are all that is needed.

Since a good proportion of the publicity effort involves getting interviews for actors and directors, pithy biographies allow for easy reference when phone pitching, and for smooth switching to another target when the journo isn't interested in the actor or the angle that's being offered. Having biographies on hand at the start of the process enables you to supply further details about a creative's credits for stories quickly, or to beef up releases that are looking a little thin. Collate them into a one or two page document that mirrors the layout of your press release for easy faxing or emailing. Biographies can also be adapted for promotional material and programs. If your publicist requests a complete CV to send to a journalist, then remove personal/agent contact details.

Make sure you also prepare a company biography, with details of the company's goals, history and achievements.

Photos

You need two sets of photos for your publicity arsenal: promotional/rehearsal shots and production shots. It's no longer possible to do without either if you are serious about gaining short and long-lead stories and reviews for your show. Thankfully, the days of expensive processing and printing are behind us; first round promotional shots can be taken using a decent digital camera, and photos can be disseminated by email.

The first photo shoot should take place about eight weeks prior to opening night. This may be difficult if the team is not fully formed, but it's easier now that the print media's photo tastes have moved away from costumed black-and-white rehearsal shots (always hard for co-operative productions) to interesting, non-rehearsal full-colour shots of actors 'on location'. The rules are that photos must only feature actors who are in the show; they should have relevance to the location or themes of the production; and they should not be 'treated' or enhanced by digital processes. Make your shots visually interesting or dynamic, with clear exposure of faces. In the absence of an interesting environment, stick to mid-shots and shots of faces in action. It's always preferable to use a professional photographer, but if you are strapped for cash, save their skills for your production shots and find a colleague who has a digital camera and a good eye.

Need some examples? For East Coast Theatre Company's production of *The Empress of China*, a few of the cast donned bits of their Chinese costumes and paraded around the Chinese Gardens at Sydney's Darling Harbour. The cast of Queensize Production's *One Flea Spare* took to Clovelly Cemetery in period costume and created some wonderfully moody photos with shadows and angles. You only need one or two great photos for your pre-show publicity strategies.

Production photos are used for reviews, follow-up promotion and archival purposes. They should be taken by a professional photographer in the final days of production week, so you have digital shots available by the day of opening. It's best if the photographer can take photos during a dress rehearsal (an experienced theatre photographer can do this without using a flash), so that the flavour and movement of the show is genuinely captured. If you wish to capture a particularly dynamic but fleeting moment, do some additional 'set-up' shots at the end of the run. Ask the photographer to burn the best twenty shots to a disc and select two or three that can be emailed to the press to accompany reviews.

Dynamic mid-shots that clearly show two or more faces are popular with press for both promotional and productions photos, as are expressive group shots that tell an interesting 'story'. Avoid sending fuzzy, 'movement streaked', overly arty or solo shots (unless it's a solo show of course!). Photos should be in full colour. Send them in jpeg format—300 dpi and 500kbs is suitable for most publications. If you have a website it's easy to set up a media section from which publicity photos can be downloaded in a range of sizes and formats. If you do this, make sure you mention it in your media release. Supply your publicist with five or six high resolution images (up to 1mb each is usually fine) on a disc. Don't bombard them with a pile of images they will have to spend time picking through. Standard promotional 'headshots' are only useful for publicists to identify actors. They are not a substitute for promotional shots, even for a solo show.

With the advent of internet publications and the use of colour photography in newspapers, it's no longer possible to promote shows without good photos. I cannot stress how important they are! I have seen many great productions miss out on fantastic media opportunities through lack of photos and more mediocre shows thrive on a single spectacular shot. If you do not arm yourself or your publicist with decent photos, choice placements that could have been yours might slip through your fingers.

Preparing angles and pitches

Pitching is just another word for talking up your production and highlighting the juiciest aspects of the play and the creative team. Once you've sent out your media release, follow up with calls to producers, editors and journalists, to check that they received your initial information. Suggest particular creatives for interviews and possible story angles. Initially these calls may be brief and the answer 'no'. You might find this off-putting, but with experience, you'll get to know the tastes of particular journalists and be able to make further suggestions if your first pitch doesn't find its target. You'll also recognise when to back off and move on. Always be polite and friendly and avoid the temptation to be pushy. Remember you are there for the long haul and your primary aim is to develop relationships that will increase in depth and value.

Before you get out and pitch, make sure you understand the strengths and weaknesses of your show in relation to media interest. Your production may seem more important to you than anything else in the world, but to the media monolith it's just one of a dozen shows that is being pitched to them at any given time. You'll also be competing for non-specific arts space, so in some instances you'll be in competition with hundreds of other artistic products.

How do you make your show stand out from the crowd? How do you grab the attention of hard-bitten arts editors with your searing social satire in a little black box, over the allure of glitzy big name extravaganzas? The good news is that a number of mainstream editors, managers and journalists love alternative fare and believe in giving newcomers and community artists a go. So fire and see where those bullets land! If your show is very 'dark', has no topical edge and features actors with low profiles, though, it will be very difficult to raise a lot of interest. And, in any case, you may well find that the local and street press and community radio, whose power is often hugely underestimated, are better outlets for your likely audience.

First, think about angles or aspects of the show that might generate interviews and stories. If you are doing it yourselves, gather the team around for a big brainstorming session. It's important (in both hired gun and DIY scenarios) to discuss the 'messages' you want to put across. Media coverage will be more cohesive if the whole team has an understanding of this. Consider:

1. **Artist profiles:** Which members of the company might be interesting subjects for interviews? Who has done what, when and where? Has your director recently completed a film, or has an actor just returned from fabulous overseas work or study? Will you have celebrity guests at your opening night that might interest the social pages?

Make a record of the suburbs where you live. Local press are often keen to print articles about residents of their communities.

2. **Topicality and newsworthiness:** Does the play connect with current affairs or matters of contemporary social interest? Has the play or playwright attracted interest overseas or in other states? Many companies overlook the possibility of pitching for a *news story*. You can only do this if your show genuinely crosses into news if, say, it is about a current war or controversial legislation or it makes news itself when it is picketed or attacked by a public figure.

3. **Company history and connections:** Does the company have a great recent track record, a penchant for unusual work, has it won awards, does it have a prominent benefactor or are company members linked (trained together, family)?

4. **Cultural or social specificity:** Are there specific groups of people the show might appeal to? Are there performers who are gay and lesbian, from diverse cultural backgrounds? Is the show about single parenthood, office culture or taxi drivers? Many cultural and social groups have organisations, newsletters and publications that offer publicity (and marketing) opportunities.

5. **Controversy, gossip and gimmicks:** Is your production hard-hitting, ground-breaking, naughty, likely to cause a heated reaction? Does a performer achieve an amazing feat within the show? If a strange or quirky event happens through the run (the resident ghost is haunting the production), offer tidbits to 'back-page' and gossip columns. These avenues are particularly good for getting the word out early as well: a snippet about an actor eating one hundred doughnuts a week can run whilst you're still in rehearsal. If you're on the hunt for an unusual prop (a Viking crossbow or a 1920s Underwood typewriter for example) see if you can get a column to do a plug.

Perhaps you have one major angle or actor to push, and a couple of back-ups that will appeal to specific parts of the media. Are there members of the team who *don't* want to be interviewed? Although this makes things harder for the team as a whole, it's vital to establish this *before* you start pitching.

When you are chasing up journalists, you should have a couple of ideas up your sleeve, in case your main drawcard isn't working. If you have pitched an angle a few times without attracting any interest, then review your approach. Throughout this occasionally demoralising process it's important to stay positive, patient, flexible and above all, realistic in your expectations. The following applies to both hired gun and do-it-yourself scenarios.

Generally, it will be easier to get stories, interviews and reviews if:

● One or more of your artists already has a media (particularly television or film) profile. The higher the profile, the more likely it is that *most* of your coverage will be generated through this one person. If this puts other noses out of joint, remind them that the publicist is not working to satisfy egos, but for the good of the whole production.

● The play is a sought-after Australian premiere, highly topical, controversial or newsworthy. It's pretty much all in the timing here.

● There is an idiosyncratic aspect to the team or show: it's staged underwater, it's a family affair or someone consumes half a ton of baked beans during the performance. You get my drift …

● The production will be performed in more than one town or state. Touring productions have a much better shot at 'national' coverage.

It will be harder to get coverage if:

● It's a frequently staged play, cast with inexperienced actors.

- A lot of shows open around the same time. When major preview opportunities get snapped up by bigger shows, getting mainstream coverage for indie productions is tough. Multiple openings in the same week (sometimes the same night) happens frequently in capital cities, and reviewers might miss opening night.
- The show lacks colour, seems dry or is short on visual impact. Visual images form a huge part of the media 'sell' to consumers. If the show *looks* interesting or sexy, it's going to help!

Out in the field

Once you're fully armed with your publicity toolkit—a pithy media release, biographical information and stand-out photos—it's time to get that publicity ball rolling! The following is a very brief and basic guide to timing your media assault, working towards opening night.

- **8–10 weeks out (from opening night)**

  Isolate 'long-range' targets such as monthly and quarterly publications and major articles or opportunities (like the Metro 'stage page'), that are booked up weeks in advance. Send out media releases (via email or fax, though email is now more common) and one or two photos where appropriate. It's hard to strike a mention in a major glossy magazine unless the play's issues are of particular interest to the publication. Great photos are a must in this instance.

  It's rare for indie shows to get television coverage except in regional areas. If your show has a particular cultural or social bent and would appeal to specific programs, then make them aware of your production now.

  Follow up with a phone call a week later to check your information has landed on the right desk. Don't waste too much time on long shots, though. Concentrate your efforts on one or two possibilities and move on if it looks unlikely.

- **5–6 weeks out**
  Do a general mail-out, fax-out or email-out of your media release to all your media contacts. Highlight major short-range targets to follow-up.

- **4–5 weeks out**
  Follow up your highlighted targets with phone calls, check that releases were received, and if more information or photos are required. Re-send releases that have been lost (a very common occurrence) and send photos on request. Pitch for interviews and stories. Place free listings.

  Identify the media (including reviewers) you wish to invite to opening night. Send out media invitations to arts editors (who allocate reviewers) and *all* theatre reviewers. Enclose a press release and flyer for the show.

- **3 weeks out**
  Check that editors have logged your opening night. If you are on friendly terms with particular reviewers, confirm they have received their invitations (by phone or email). Mail out general opening night invitations. Continue to chase preview stories and interviews.

- **2 weeks out**
  Continue to chase preview stories and reviewers. Lock down street and local press interviews. Organise any photo shoots. You might also like to do a 'second-wave' media release email to secondary media.

- **1 week out**
  Organise and attend interviews. Lock down reviewers and assess opening night RSVPs. Follow-up key invitees where appropriate or close off and create a waiting list. Prepare media kits. Follow up social press if appropriate.

- **Production week and opening night**
  Organise and attend interviews. Take production shots and burn to disc. Set-up media desk and schmooze!
- **Post-opening**
  Check review release dates, and chase editors if appropriate. Keep pushing opportunities for spotlighting the show in 'what's on' and 'back page' columns. Are there any more radio opportunities?

Through this entire period you hope to be logging lots of interviews, connecting journalists with actors, directors and writers, and making sure that your company members have full details of interview contacts, times and locations. Set-up a communication system that allows interview details to be relayed to the appropriate people *in writing*, with copies going to your rehearsal room stage manager. If journalists are contacting creatives directly, ask them to cc you a copy of the interview details, so that you are aware of all media activity. Always call creatives the night before an interview to check they have correct details and call them post-interview to see how it went. If you have a good relationship with the interviewer, you might also call them the following day to check if further information or additional photos are required. If you have time, it is a good relationship-developing exercise to accompany creatives to major interviews or photo shoots.

It's most important that all requests for interview set-ups and further information and photos are attended to promptly. If you are the nominated publicist, then it's vital that you are easy to contact, and attend to details without fuss. Opportunities sometimes come up unexpectedly, and if you're not on the ball, they'll be happily snapped up by someone else.

Soon it will be time to pull out your very best foyer skills, and delight people with your opening night charm. We'll deal with opening night media and reviewers a bit more in Chapter 9.

7

Dollars and sense

Bankrolling your production

One of the most significant commitments you will make to a company or a production, aside from your time, effort and dedication, will be your money. Few independent productions manage to get off the ground without some out-of-pocket investment by company members.

There are alternatives to forking out lots of your own money, but your success at garnering funding, investment or sponsorship from outside sources will depend on a number of factors such as the lead-time you have, the artistic nature of the work and the profile of artists, your knowledge of financial sources, useable contacts within the company and the ability to put together good proposals. You should also be mindful of the fact that money sourced from government, philanthropists and sponsors is rarely given without strings. You must be sure that you can meet any obligations before running off with the booty.

Once you have created a budget for the production, you should isolate 'up-front' costs. Expenditure might amount to $12,000, but $5000 will get the ball rolling. While costs for marketing materials, venue deposits and advances for rights are needed immediately, other items can wait until box office income starts rolling in. If you don't have a lot of cash to start with and defer payments until the production starts generating income, however, make sure that you are *very* realistic about income. It's one thing to lose an initial investment when the production doesn't generate as much income as planned, and quite another to end up with a swag of bills that you cannot pay.

Personal contributions

The upside of using your own money to fuel shows is that there are no strings attached. The downside is that you'll be pouring hard-earned cash from an already financially-challenged lifestyle into an uncertain venture with almost no chance of monetary gain. Sound like madness? Well, a lot of companies and producers do precisely this, but the smart ones plan to get their investment back. The rule of thumb is that, unless you are prepared to sacrifice savings for a potentially career altering role or a genuine labour of love, only invest if there is a good chance that your 'loan' will be returned to you through the box office. Of course even with the best intentions and planning this can't be guaranteed, but if you budget expenditure meticulously (and stick to it) and you are realistic about potential income, you should be able to assess the risk. Take into account the venue profile, the efficiency of your production team and, if you are not the primary producer, the experience of the individual who will be monitoring budgets and cash flow. It's generally a good idea to act as producer or co-producer when your own money is invested, to keep your finger on the pulse.

Often the core members of an indie company share the investment which is managed by the producer. This creates a sense of egalitarianism and, because they have put in money, it encourages everyone to take responsibility for promoting the show through their personal networks. In this situation you need to ensure that the producer is efficient, and that everyone has agreed to the budgets before any money is spent. All financial arrangements should be specifically detailed in the co-op's contract or Letter of Agreement.

Government funding

Garnering grants from funding bodies can be hard slog for smaller indie companies with limited experience, but there is no reason why talented groups with a track record shouldn't start building relationships with funding bodies. I am still amazed by the fear that the idea of dealing with arts bureaucracies strikes into the hearts of young artists. I am constantly told by indie groups, 'We'd have no chance against more experienced artists'; 'The whole grant process is a mystery to me'; 'it's so much paperwork for probably no return'; 'we just can't plan that far ahead'. I'm more amazed when funding body project managers say to me, 'We are really interested in some of the great work on the independent scene—why aren't more indie groups applying?'

Part of the reason for this conundrum seems to be the inability of funding bodies to track the complex and constantly shifting web of indie companies and partnerships. This prevents them from 'demystifying' themselves by getting information directly to tiny companies; although they sometimes use more established companies and industry networks to help them do this. It's also partly the failure of young artists to seek information proactively; to make themselves aware of opportunities, to pick up handbooks and scour websites, to talk to artform project managers before applying, and to be brave enough to ask for help from senior practitioners. My advice to talented young companies is to take the bull by the horns and get over their fear of all things funding. Dive into those handbooks and websites and you may well be surprised at the transparency of many funding systems, the amount of effort that has gone into making it as easy as possible for artists to understand core values and criteria and the advice available on how to articulate the details of your projects.

A brief word here on the difference between administration and boards or committees. Government funding bodies have employees (program managers and officers) who, in their various capacities, administer, research, make policy and facilitate funding processes. Board or committee members are drawn from the artistic community and generally serve for a set period. These industry practitioners can be involved with policy-making and the development of initiatives, but they are primarily responsible for assessing applications and making funding decisions, with the support of the administrative staff.

Indie companies are right to think that competition for funding at all levels is fierce; in truth there is never enough money to fund more than a small fraction of the yearly ask in each state and at federal level. It's also true that you may have to apply a number of times before you achieve a small success (and if your work isn't exciting you may not get there at all), and it is a time-consuming and sometimes heart-breaking process. There are four things that indie companies can do to maximize their efforts and increase their chances of getting a berth on the funding train:

1. **Know what's out there:** Your first task is to pick up handbooks or guidelines for your relevant state or territory **[W34]** funding body and the federal body, the Australia Council for the Arts **[W27]** and to plough through these and their accompanying websites. I strongly recommend that you bookmark these websites and make it a habit to browse them for announcements, initiative updates and new links every couple of weeks. Make sure you also check out your local council for community cultural programs and grants. Councils often have small grants (generally up to $5000) for not-for-profit groups who enhance the cultural life of the community.

   I've provided web addresses for each major state funding body in the web directory, but with internet access it's really easy (and fun) to discover a myriad of grants and services offered by both government and non-government sectors. The 'links' pages for state body websites are comprehensive guides to many other organisations and funding opportunities—once you get started on the chain of web links, you'll be amazed at what you discover. Artsinfo **[W35]** (no longer updated but it still has useful links) and the Culture and Recreation Portal **[W36]** which includes a comprehensive online grants and services finder **[W37]**, both developed by the Department of Communications, Information Technology and the Arts (DCITA) will help you to begin a comprehensive journey of reading and research.

Aside from information about their grants programs, many government sites provide access to invaluable information and resources. It's easy to demystify these towering organisations for yourselves by clicking through their news and research centres; in particular, the Australia Council provides access to extensive reviews, working papers and reports on the state of the arts across a number of years. You'll also find links to marvellous (and free) marketing resources such as fuel4arts.com **[W28]** and The Program **[W38]**.

2. **Aim for targets within your reach:** Once you've done some careful research, you will get a feel for eligible grants for your company. Skip through annual and triennial grant sections and look at one-off program grants and development initiatives. Make sure that you read *all* categories and not just theatre since you may find an additional category that's relevant to your work. Perhaps your project is hybrid in nature or has new media content. For your first grant, unless you've made a huge public splash with some brilliant and ground-breaking work that *everyone* is talking about, start small. It's rare for funding bodies to hand over significant amounts of cash to new companies, but it's not uncommon for

them to take a chance on an exciting project that needs a few thousand dollars for the first stage development of a new work.

It's often easier for new companies to get grants through state bodies, which have a particular interest in the development of artists in their region. There's a better chance that the company's work has been seen by a fund member, and you'll be competing at state/territory rather then federal level. Australia Council (or Ozco) rounds are the toughest as one key criteria is 'artistic innovation' (which can be hard to prove when you are in the early stages of development) and you'll be competing with experienced artists from around the country. Still, if you have a genuinely innovative project it's possible to get over the line. But once again, start modestly. If you're new to the game, apply first for a creative development grant. If that goes well, apply for further funding in a second or third application.

Funding bodies also create strategic development initiatives, which are basically non-permanent categories created to target specific areas or to respond quickly to current trends. Many address the needs of emerging and regional artists and you should scour websites for these opportunities. At the time of writing, the Young Artists Initiative from the Australia Council is enabling companies with members mostly under the age of 26 to get significant 'New Work' grants through its Theatre Fund. If you are working in the regions, check out Regional Arts Australia **[W39]** which is a national body supporting the arts in regional and remote areas, together with individual state peak bodies. There are also a number of organisations to assist touring at regional, state and national levels, which we'll look at in Chapter 10.

Individuals should look carefully at fellowships and scholarships as well as Skills and Arts Development categories at both state and federal levels. The British Council **[W40]**, the UK's agency for international cultural relations, also provides undergraduate and post-graduate scholarships for young artists wishing to train at arts institutions in the UK.

3. **Talk to people who know:** Once you've worked out which grant to go for, download the application form and list anything you don't clearly understand. Before you apply, talk to a project officer at the funding organisation—there is usually at least one assigned to each artform or category (contacts are easily found on websites). Many companies make the mistake of applying without checking out details and inexperienced artists may apply to a category for which they are not eligible, thus wasting time and effort. A simple phone call to a program manager or officer will soon get you on the right track. In my experience, program managers and officers care a great deal about the arts (they are often from an arts background themselves), they are friendly and helpful individuals and they know the grant processes backwards. Remember, these people do not make funding decisions and have no hidden agenda; they are there to make sure you have the right category in mind, and to answer any questions you may have about the process.

If you are interested in grants, invite fund committee members (decision-makers) to your productions throughout the year. Names of the current committee are available from the relevant website and unless you have personal or work addresses, you should mail invitations care of the funding body. Send invites to all state funding body committee members and to your state representative for the Australia Council. They may not have time to attend your shows, but it's a good idea to add them to your invitation lists, so they remain informed of your general progress.

If you are a first or second-time applicant, don't submit an application without showing it to a *successful* grant applicant first. This means giving yourself plenty of time to prepare, write and revise your submission. Don't leave it to the last minute! A couple of weeks before the deadline, run it past a mentor, a senior practitioner, a season hub curator or manager who supports your work (or who is perhaps prepared to auspice the grant). They will be able to correct obvious mistakes, point out omissions and comment on project articulation.

4. **Follow-up on failures:** If your application is unsuccessful, it's easy to fall into a depression and imagine all sorts of reasons for missing out. But you may have been closer to the finish line than you think. Before you let your imagination take hold, give your project officer a call and ask if they have any notes from the funding meeting that might be useful. You won't get specific feedback in every instance, but if the project survived the initial cut and was discussed by the committee, it's very likely that your project officer can tell you its basic strengths and weaknesses. This process can be extremely helpful when you rework your approach for a (successful) second application. A lot of young artists and companies are shy of asking for feedback—don't be! It's a great way to learn about what you are doing right and wrong. What can you lose except the cost of a phone call?

Philanthropy

Philanthropy is the practice of providing charitable aid and donations. There are many corporations, trusts, foundations and individuals who give generously to the arts industry each year. Opportunities for small companies are limited as most are geared towards organisations that have legal, non-profit and Gift Deductible Receipt (GDR) status. Funding opportunities for individuals are available for research, scholarships, fellowships and travel grants. You need to sift carefully to determine the specific purposes of the trusts as well as priority interests, geographic specificity, and notable exclusions.

Philanthropy Australia **[W41]** is the national philanthropic body, and represents private, family, corporate and community grant-makers in Australia. Their Australian Directory of Philanthropy provides contact details for hundreds of Australian Trusts and Foundations (for a range of sectors, not just the arts) and is well worth the investment of around $100 for online access (or less for a hard copy). They have developed services for grant seekers including workshops and fact sheets on their comprehensive website.

The Ian Potter Foundation **[W42]** is one of Australia's largest philanthropic foundations and makes grants for general charitable purposes including the arts. Organisations need GDR status to apply to the Foundation, but the affiliated Ian Potter Cultural Trust **[W43]** makes small grants (up to $5000) to individuals in the early stage of their careers.

The Australian Business Arts Foundation **[W44]** is a Commonwealth–owned company supported by DCITA. Its aim is to increase private sector support for the arts by 'introducing' cultural sector participants to the business sector (and vice versa), and helping them to form mutually beneficial partnerships. The Foundation works with established companies, but their website is a great place to start dreaming of a bigger, brighter future.

Fundraising events

The average fundraising drive for an indie production consists of an entertainment 'event' promoted amongst colleagues, friends and family. Charging a modest ticket price, the company hosts bands and acts, holds a raffle and gives out donated door prizes. This can be a very tough way for companies to raise money. It's time-consuming and you need several people devoted to the task to achieve good results. I've seen groups put as much effort into mounting fundraisers as they do getting productions off the ground, reaping only a small financial return and exhausting themselves in the process.

Before you commit yourself to a groovy event, carefully weigh up the pros and cons. Ask yourselves:

- Can you get the venue for free? (often easier on traditionally slow nights). Will you have exclusive use of the room? Until what time?
- Will you need to put money on the bar to make tickets more attractive to supporters? If so, can you negotiate drink prices for the first hour of the evening? If not, can you bring in sponsored alcohol (champagne cocktails perhaps) for an icebreaker round?
- Do you have enough contacts to procure decent door and raffle prizes through donations?
- Can you get enough great (and reliable) entertainment and an experienced MC together? Will you need to bring in sound or lighting equipment?
- Do you have enough company members, friends or colleagues (not involved with the production) who are willing to help with marketing the event, gathering prizes and setting up raffles? Will there be enough people to 'work' the room on the night, to sell tickets at the door and walk around spruiking raffle tickets and collecting donations?
- Do you have a big enough network of supporters to buy enough tickets to make it all worth while?

Creating a fundraising event is akin to putting on a show, and for small teams it's hard to do both at once with limited resources. On the positive side, a really memorable event can create a sense of well-earned camaraderie and a great buzz about the show. It also gives you the opportunity to distribute promotional material and ticket offers throughout the night. Do your sums carefully in the planning stages and if you're not going to make at least $1500–$2000 profit, then reconsider the whole thing.

Most indie companies mount these ventures without much thought for the legalities of it all. Legislation differs between states, and if you are doing some serious fundraising with the general public you need to be aware of it. I have included URLs for state authorities in the Web Directory [W45]. It may seem simple to run a raffle, but there are a number of requirements and restrictions. (In NSW for example, you must comply with the Lotteries and Arts Union Act and if your prizes include alcohol, you can't sell tickets to persons under the age of eighteen.)

Sponsorship

A sponsor is an individual or organisation that partners a company or a production, supporting it either financially or through the provision of goods and services. 'Partner' is the operative word here. Sponsorship deals generally require that the production company offers something in return.

Major arts organisations have staff, and often entire departments, devoted to 'development', people who negotiate complex activity for their organisations. They propose ideas for cash and in-kind support for shows, tours and other company activities to the corporate sector and ensure that sponsorship benefits are properly delivered. Major arts companies will often have a network of supporters in place, ranging from smaller-scale sponsors offering free or discounted goods and services (such as paper for printing or flowers for opening nights and functions), through cash partners for individual productions, to the top-tier—the major corporate partners who give substantial amounts of cash that support a company's entire season.

Sponsorship development for the independent sector is tough territory. If you enter into it, you need to be sure that you are able to 'service' any sponsor agreements (arts organisations often have one person to secure sponsors and another to look after them). You also

Luke Mullins and Jessamy Dyer in the Stuck Pigs Squealing production of *The Eisteddfod* for The Store Room. Photo: Vivian Cooper Smith

need to make sure that it doesn't end up costing you money. A lot of indie companies fall over themselves to get someone on board for a tiny sum, only to find the hundred tickets they gave the sponsor in return would have garnered them twice as much income through the box office for their sell-out show. Still, learning to write good proposals, to pitch smoothly to the business and corporate world and to foster relationships that may grow with your company can be hugely productive and rewarding. Develop proposals carefully, so that you are comfortable communicating with and, in some cases, involving partners in your work, and ensure you can 'look after' your sponsors as you have agreed.

Whom to approach

Indie companies simply don't have the size, profile or promotional power to interest major corporations which want to reach large audiences and/or align themselves with prestige arts activity. One of the most significant benefits a company offers is a 'branding' opportunity, which may help a sponsor to promote itself to a particular demographic, or to offer benefits to its corporate clients (through tickets and functions), or simply to enhance its profile as a good corporate citizen. So ask yourself: is your controversial indie show in an 80-seat non-air-conditioned venue a good match for a major telecommunication network with merchant banking clients? If show tickets are the core feature of your sponsor packages, it makes sense to seek out sponsors who, aside from their interest in supporting quirky, small-scale, innovative work, may also want to see it, or have clients who do. This certainly does not mean that bigger corporations are out of reach, but look for opportunities at a local rather than national level, and think about pitching for support in the form of goods in kind, rather than cash.

Sponsorship negotiations are based on relationship building and can be slow. It can take months for a decision to be made. Cash is particularly hard to get without much lead time if you are a small company just starting to build a profile. Consider focusing on contra instead. Try selling nights at the theatre (a ticket/drink/meet the cast package for instance) rather than asking for a big sponsorship amount.

When seeking 'matches' for cash or in-kind support, or simply for dissemination of promotional material through staff networks and newsletters (a contribution not to be underestimated), consider:

● Who do you know? Many successful development partnerships (both at fringe and mainstream levels), have started with a personal contact; someone that an artistic director or development manager drinks or plays netball with. When you put the production together, you should ask *every* company member, core or otherwise, if they have any relatives, friends or general contacts who may be able to help with a proposal or provide a personal introduction to an organisation. This could be an 'in' to a larger business that might otherwise disregard your proposal. Don't be shy. Even professional development managers hate 'going in cold', and I suspect that only a small proportion of successful corporate partnerships have been initiated blindly.

Whilst we're on the subject of personal connections, let's also talk briefly about network-building. Arts circles have a fairly small radius. If you're only socialising with other arts participants, your personal networks are bound to be small. Producers need to get out there. Do you play sport or take courses? Are you a member of any associations or community groups that are *not* associated with theatre or the performing arts? Like-minded individuals can be found in many other sectors and, apart from having fun (and finding relief from the stress of mounting indie shows), you may find potential supporters and investors in your growing sphere of influence!

- Is there a feature of your production or company that might appeal to a specific business, corporate sector or company? Is the show about taxi-drivers, hairdressers, bankers, or a particular cultural group? If your production has a negative spin on a particular industry, though, it may be a hard sell!

- Be honest about the nature of your production, particularly if it includes nudity, lots of colourful language, or a strong political agenda. When a big company makes sponsorship decisions they will generally err on the side of caution rather than risk—they don't want to make their clients uncomfortable. If there is any part of the production that might offend you need to let potential sponsors know beforehand.

● Does the show deal with an issue or cause that is supported by a particular community outreach program? For example, if a corporation has pledged money to community literacy programs, support for homeless young people or the prevention of cruelty to animals, and your show is about one of those issues, then they might be worth approaching. If cash or in-kind support is not forthcoming, ask if they are willing to distribute information about the show through their staff and community partner networks.

● Are there props and consumables in your production that could be donated through in-kind support? If a script demands the consumption of a kilo of spaghetti during each performance, in-kind sponsorship could save you hundreds of dollars on one item alone. If it's a big company, this can sometimes be as hard as getting cash. Try approaching a local shop or the distributor rather than the manufacturer.

● Printing sponsorship deals are definitely worth more than the paper they're printed on. Make sure you consider the paper too! Start developing relationships with local printers and paper suppliers. Printed marketing materials are one of biggest up-front costs that an indie company has, and even a small discount, in return for an ad in the program and a few tickets, can save heaps of dollars. If your negotiations for full sponsorship are unsuccessful, ask if they will offer a discount.

● Match size for size. If you're a small operation, then approach small businesses or shops, rather than a manufacturer or head office. It can be very hard to get to the decision-makers of national corporations. For big organisations pitch at 'branch' rather than national level if you can. If you approach smaller businesses, you'll be dealing with less hierarchy (and sometimes directly with the decision-maker) and can track the progress of your proposal more effectively. Local businesses are often willing to support local product, since it's an investment in their community and a way of promoting themselves to it.

- Think hard about the profile and personality of your production; is it funky and full of hot young things? Arty and serious with a mix of younger and more established artists? Or is it lightweight, irreverent and fun? What businesses or organisations would like to be associated with your personality and 'vibe'?
- Think equally as hard about the profile, interests and lifestyle of patrons it might attract, as this is not only your target audience, but the demographic for potential sponsors. You can then promote your target audience to relevant business sectors.

Proposals

If you are pitching to the business or corporate sector develop a strongly-written proposal. Most independent companies make the mistake of incorporating every single detail about their history and artistic dreams in reams of unstructured, long-winded rambling. Keep your proposal to two pages. Think of it as a funding application; be clear, stick to the facts and use historical or biographical information as support material that can be read separately.

Think carefully about what you can offer sponsors. Promotional and marketing opportunities, including logo and ad placements and distribution of promotional materials, along with tickets to performances are the most obvious. Remember, though, that tickets are a valuable commodity, so try to structure packages that don't deprive you of too much income. Previews are often hard to sell, so rather than 'papering' randomly, why not use large numbers (or a whole house) of preview tickets for sponsors? You can set up a low-key function with an opportunity to meet the cast on the night without much difficulty or expense. Let the major sponsor speak over drinks and perhaps give them a signed and framed poster of the show to make them feel included. You could also offer discount or concession-rate tickets to staff (confine this to the quieter nights if you think the show will sell well). Offer some opening night tickets (four maximum for a small venue). Corporate sponsors often like to use tickets to entertain their own clients and guests (which is why it's so important to get the 'match' right); perhaps you can offer a limited number of in-season tickets to principal sponsors.

If you are working within a season hub or a larger venue, you need to check that you are not targeting sponsors that will clash with any venue or season sponsors. It would be very embarrassing to offer logo placement in a foyer, only to discover (after you've signed an agreement), that this is the exclusive precinct of a venue sponsor. It's worth noting the contentious nature of alcohol sponsors. They are often the easiest to interest (many will even offer cash), as they benefit by getting their product exposed in a new location or sold at a new bar. Yet many venues already have restrictive alcohol deals in place, and may not be able to accommodate competitive distributors, even if they are offering sponsored alcohol for opening night.

A lot of companies make the mistake of sending out vague proposals that offer every possible benefit they can think of to potential sponsors, without any dollar value attached. It's much more sensible to create levels of support, with a range of benefits listed alongside the dollars it will take to procure them. Create incentives for sponsors to upgrade to the next sponsorship level. Never send out proposals without prices—the target of your proposal will be much more comfortable if you include dollar expectations. For example:

- **Level one: Production Partner—$5000+** (A company who contributes cash, services or goods to the value of $5000+)
  - Exclusive position as Production Partner with prominent placement of logo on all marketing and media materials, advertising and programs

- Half page ad in program
- Major presenting credit (Flying Pigs and Lion Upholstery present...)
- Distribution of your promotional material through a direct mail-out of 3000, twice-weekly seat-drops and distribution of sample bags where appropriate
- 20 tickets to the preview performance with complimentary programs, post-show drinks, and an opportunity to speak at our post-preview function
- 4 tickets to opening night and 10 in-season double passes
- Specially discounted tickets for staff

- **Level two: Production Stars—$3000+** (A company who contributes cash, services or goods to the value of $3000+). There is a limit of two Production Stars:
  - Placement of logo on all marketing and media materials, advertising and programs
  - One quarter-page ad in program
  - Distribution of your promotional material through a direct mail-out of 3000
  - 10 tickets to preview and complimentary programs and post-show drinks
  - 2 tickets to opening night and 10 in-season-double passes
  - Tickets at concession rate for all staff

- **Level three: Production Buddies—$1000+** (A company who contributes cash, services or goods to the value of $1000+). There is a limit of three Production Buddies.
  - Placement of logo on flyers and programs
  - 10 x 2 ad in program
  - 4 tickets to preview, complimentary programs and post-show drinks
  - 2 tickets to opening night

- Tickets at concession rate for all staff
- You could also have an incentive tier for individuals (Production Friends) who contribute between $100 and $500:
  - 2 double in-season passes, complimentary programs and post-show drinks
  - Acknowledgment in program

The art of grabbing the reader via an expertly written proposal can take many years to master. There is a myriad of book and web resources available that can help you hone your skills, but a simple and direct approach can also work wonders. Here are a few basic tips on preparing and structuring a proposal:

- Personalise it. Don't write a proposal until you have made contact with the organisation and know who you are writing for. Once you've made contact with the right person, do a sales pitch on the phone and let them know to expect your proposal. *Never* send out a proposal without finding out the *name* of your target. A letter to 'Dear Madam/Sir' will go straight in the bin. Tailor the pitch to the specific entity, even if you're just subtly modifying your basic document. Blanket distribution of proposals will have the same effect as using exactly the same letter to apply for ten different jobs. None at all!
- Put yourself in the potential sponsor's shoes. What would you want to know about the show if you had to ascertain the benefits for your company and make the decision to contribute or not? Think 'Who, What, When, and most importantly, Why?'

  Start with the obvious: who you are and what you are doing. Follow with a brief paragraph clearly describing the show, venue, dates and number of performances. If there are great people associated with the production, mention them here. If you have some information about your target audience, include some relevant quotes about audience demographics.

- Outline the different levels of support and highlight the benefits of each: 'The incredible level of exposure and entertaining benefits that *only* a Production Partner receives'. Create incentives for sponsors to consider upgrading to a higher level of investment.
- In a paragraph or a few dot points, try to nail what it is about this partnership that is unique; quintessentially, why they would want to come on board. You can talk about profile and entertaining opportunities, audience demographic, or community presence. Do some research about the organisation (mission statements, community interests etc), so that if you have similar goals and aims, you can point this out in the proposal.

  Finish off with a brief company history, an outline of company goals or a few lines about the potential of the 'relationship', and remember to supply contact details.
- Additional information such as marketing plans, detailed distribution or audience demographic information, company history, artist biographies and past reviews or commentaries can be supplied in additional pages as support material.

Following up

Don't sit around waiting for potential sponsors to respond to your proposal—they won't. Even when you have made personal contact, you will find that you are continually doing the chasing. This is completely normal, so be patient, polite and persistent. Don't sound desperate; a sponsor will value your product more highly if you value it yourself!

A couple of days after mailing or emailing your proposal, call to check that your contact has received it. If they give you a timeframe for assessing it, then call back at the appropriate time to ask if you can arrange a meeting, or if they would like more information. Until you get a definite 'no', continue to chase a meeting or decision at suitable intervals (that don't constitute harassment!). If it's a big organisation it may take time to get a real response, so make sure you allow a few months.

If you are lucky enough to find a sponsor, make sure that you put together a letter of agreement, outlining the details of your partnership. This is important. It can be a simple one-page letter or an outline that is signed by both parties, but it should clearly state expectations for both sides.

Make sure that your company has agreed to everything you offer and that someone is dedicated to delivering the benefits you've promised. Most importantly, *don't ever* promise something you can't deliver or over which you have no control (such as media mentions of sponsors).

Once you have a sponsor or sponsors on board, it's vital that you look after them as you have agreed. Limited time and resources and the stresses of putting on a low-budget indie production are no excuse for failing to live up to your end of the bargain. Ignoring or forgetting to inform sponsors of events will destroy the potential for an ongoing relationship, and may also put a sponsor off dealing with the sector in general, which has an impact on the wider artistic community.

Finally, make sure that you thank your contributors properly. A card and gift basket, a framed poster signed by the cast together with a memento pack containing photos and reviews, will show you value your sponsors.

A lot of indie companies ask, 'Is it possible to ask the same sponsor to support us more than once?'. The answer to this is an unequivocal 'yes', provided you have met your obligations and have thanked them adequately. If it's been a mutually productive relationship, there is every reason that a sponsor might wish to continue it. It just may be the start of a beautiful friendship!

8

Step right up!

Sales and spruiking

The first seven chapters have focused on preparation and 'building'. Now, as you stand at the crown of an enormous hill and prepare to enjoy the easier gradient, it's exhilarating. At this point in your journey, you'll exchange the bulldozer for a pair of fast skates. Beware though of the hairy bends ahead. Managing speed (not just obstacles) will become one of your biggest challenges.

The *feeling* that you have to hang onto the reins more tightly as you approach your opening will be more intensified the less prepared you are. Selling your show should not be part of this downhill run, it is best addressed when you are putting together your marketing, publicity and sponsorship plans. Tackle this early and it will reduce the skidding effect on the bends. Time-critical tasks like preparing for production week, chasing media, sending out invitations, managing RSVPs, planning functions and setting up a booking system start to pile up in the final stages, so plan your sales strategies early to avoid a major collision of tasks.

A common mistake among indie companies is to make the creation of their show more important than the selling of it. This may sound sacrilegious but, in truth, it's heartbreaking to invest mind, body and soul in a wonderful work, and take the trouble to develop great artwork and good sponsor relations, if no-one, other than an enthusiastic opening night crowd, comes.

I have seen many a company triumph in front of a full house on opening night, only to realise (as they enjoy a post-opening drink) that there isn't an audience for the second, third and fourth nights. 'Forgetting' to sell your show is right up there with leaving your baby on the bus. Don't rely on word-of-mouth and reviews to do all the selling for you. Word-of-mouth only works when there are enough 'mouths' to make a noise, and if the reviews aren't good and they *precede* your sales pitch to friends and the general public, it will make your job harder. Look again at Chapter 3, where we discussed selling and anti-selling points, in the context of realistic budgeting.

For the most part, your box office income will rely on single ticket sales, which is the *most difficult* sales territory. Furthermore, indie audiences don't like booking too far ahead; it's a sector where shows can come together very quickly and the audience pretty much matches that spontaneous dynamic. Many patrons don't buy tickets more than ten days out from an event, so marketing and sales drives in the two weeks leading into a season are critical. Younger fringe patrons who are less cashed up will often wait to hook into word-of-mouth or reviews before buying a ticket.

Have you ever wondered why the first weeks of mainstream shows are so heavily booked prior to reviews and before much is known about the production? These companies don't have magic at their disposal, but they invest a great deal of time and energy (and quite a few market research dollars) in the growth and maintenance of subscription bases. Patrons who buy ticket packages receive substantial discounts and other incentives (such as free programs or drinks, show debriefings, discounts for goods and services). They are encouraged to subscribe to guarantee good seats (single tickets sales are generally closed off until the first wave of subscription sales is concluded) and they are booked in to the first few weeks of season shows. With early houses full of subscribers, sales will hopefully gain momentum, so that when single ticket sales need to kick in, the crossover should be seamless. If a show has not been well-received, the marketing department braces itself for a significant drop in houses at the crossover point, and will be madly creating strategies (including ticket deals to various sectors and organisations) to get through the rest of the season.

Few season hubs have developed a subscription base, however, and very few indie outfits attempt this. It's hard for them to service a subscriber base effectively, particularly when the mainstream now offers some remarkable ticket packages for 'under 30s', including lots of flashy incentives and bonuses. Independent shows, with their short seasons, have to hit the right note from the top of the season, an extremely difficult task.

In the absence of a subscriber comfort zone, independent companies fare best when they implement some middle-ground incentives. It's possible to build early houses up to a comfortable 40–50% through ticket deals to patrons who have supported previous shows, friends, family and colleagues and targeted papering (the practice of using complimentary tickets to pad houses). If, over a few shows, your ticket deals are focused, and loyal patrons realise there are no cheap tickets later in the season, they will start to appreciate that it's worth getting in early. It may be tempting to rely on the success of a previous show or the grunt of a season hub to get you through early performances, but such tenuous supports offer no guarantee your current show will take off. You may have a core to draw on, but audiences generally respond to small shows on a case-by-case basis. It is better to build on 40% houses of discounted tickets than to anticipate a house of full-payers, and find you have a vacancy rate of 70%. A discounted seat is always better than an empty seat, provided you approach discounts in the right way.

Sales strategies for indie shows running three to four weeks should, for the most be part, be directed at the first week-and-a-half of the show. The first three or four shows after opening night are the most vulnerable, but the first and second shows of the *second* week should also be addressed, as reviews (assuming they are good) will probably only help from the middle of this week.

Let's say you have a four week season (including production week bump-in) at a 100 seat venue. The show previews on a Wednesday, opens on a Thursday and plays Tuesday to Sunday. Papering, ticket deals, discount and full-price sales will obviously vary from show to show depending on your networks, but a typical strategy might be:

- **Preview (Wednesday):** 50% papering through student initiatives, 30% papering for sponsors, 10% papering for colleagues offering feedback, 10% sales at preview rates. Whatever breakdown is appropriate to you, aim to fill previews.
- **Opening night (Thursday):** 100% invited house (media and VIP guests) or 90% invited house and 10% sales. Aim to fill the house.
- **Shows three–five (Friday–Sunday):** 30% discount sales through early-bird mail-out to friends, family and company supporters, 20% papering through media giveaways. Aim for 50% capacity before single ticket sales at regular prices.
- **Shows six–seven (Tuesday & Wednesday week two):** 20% discount sales through offers to students and industry, 10% papering through media giveaways. Aim for 30% capacity before single ticket sales at regular prices.

Some shows will require very little or no papering and more 'difficult' pieces may need additional boosting in the early stages. Take an educated guess at what you'll need and follow a plan so you can avoid panic papering and discounting at the last minute.

Candy Bowers, Desan Padayachee, Lucy Taylor, James Lugton, Elaine Hudson and Luc Anthony in Queensize Production's *In the Blood* for B Sharp. Photo: Brett Boardman

Ticket prices

If you're working in a season hub, most likely ticket prices will be standardised for the season, but if you've hired a venue, you'll need to create a set of prices yourself. Get some advice from the venue, and research ticket prices for similar-sized shows in your town or city. If you're not sure what to do, take the prices for three or four other indie shows in your area and go for the average. Don't price below the norm unless your show is a student work, or a work-in-progress, or the venue is makeshift or doesn't offer a reasonable level of facilities or comfort. If you are a hot company with an excellent product to sell, the length of the show shouldn't affect prices too much either. Despite the odd complaint I've had about the brevity of some B Sharp shows, my experience is that most people are happier to pay for fifty minutes of thought-provoking work than two-and-half hours of tedium. It's also unwise to inflate prices dramatically. If patrons are used to paying within a certain range for indie shows, they may be put off by exceptional prices unless the reason is very clear to them (and in their minds, worth paying for).

A typical pricing structure might be: Adult: $27, Concession: $21, Groups of ten or more: $23. It's a good idea to offer a preview discount (maybe $18). Make sure that you are clear about who is entitled to a concession *before* you start selling tickets. Will *all* students be entitled to concession prices or are international students excluded? Is there a concession rate for unemployed people and for industry, such as card-carrying members of MEAA and AWG? Will you draw a big industry crowd? If you are worried about the loss of revenue, consider setting the industry price between the adult and concession prices (maybe $24). Some venues advertise one or two special 'industry nights', which may include some other incentive such as a free drink and some nibblies.

If you are working in an established venue that takes bookings for you, remember to factor ticket handling fees (THF) into your ticket prices. Venues may also collect GST on your behalf. A THF (around $1–$3 for small venues) basically helps to cover the cost of running a box office service. It may be part of your contract that the venue is the exclusive sales point for tickets, but even if you have the choice, it's well worth the cost to have professional staff take on the onerous task of answering calls, printing tickets, managing sales and patrons. If you can set your own ticket prices, simply make sure that your prices, less THF and GST, cover your own needs.

When you are budgeting you will want to determine an 'average ticket price' (ATP). If you are mathematically inclined, you can attempt to predict the expected ratio of adult to concession-rate and group booking customers, but, as a rule of thumb, extract ticket handling fees and GST from the adult and concession rates, add what's left together and divide by two. Using this crude method, the ATP for prices shown above would be about $19.80 (assuming a THF of $2 per ticket and 10% GST).

'Pay-what-you-can' performances

A few years ago, a couple of small venues started trialling this system on their slowest night. They ditched their regular pricing schedule for one performance a week (often Monday or Tuesday) and asked each patron to pay what they could afford. The venues soon found a loyal audience and even decent box office income; whilst economically-challenged patrons pay a few dollars, others chose to pay considerably more.

In a pay-what-you-can performance, tickets cannot be pre-booked—patrons simply queue up one to two hours before the performance time. The ongoing effects and benefits of the system are yet to be determined. I've seen them work particularly well for shows that appeal to students and industry, and they are a great way to enhance targeted promotion to these audiences. An alternative is to consider a minimum price: brand your night 'Tight-wad Wednesday' or 'El Cheapo Night' and ask for a donation of at least $10. This is a strong incentive for new, tentative or cash-poor patrons.

If you decide to do this, you can put a certain percentage (20–30%) of tickets on sale at normal prices for patrons who want to book rather queue up. Don't be tempted to raise this percentage if the show is really popular; there is nothing worse than having a hundred people queue up to buy twenty available tickets. It isn't fair to advertise such as scheme without making a good proportion of your tickets available for it.

Ticketing deals and discounts

As I've previously suggested, discount deals can be advantageous or counter-productive depending on your approach. Used to promote your show in a positive way, they get word out early and fill awkward gaps in the auditorium. As a last minute-device they are much less effective; at their worst they can turn people off seeing the show. Tickets are a *valuable* commodity and giving them away willy-nilly will reduce their value in the public eye. When you are devising audience incentive strategies, consider the following:

- Discounts and incentives should be factored into your marketing plan. First identify the performances that may be hard to fill. This may include some first-week houses, a weeknight that's known to be slow for a particular venue or location, public holidays during the season, or special events that may reduce audiences (sporting finals, parades etc). Work on bolstering these weak areas.

- Devise a matrix of discounts that work together rather than against each other. Don't send two different offers to the same group of people. If you are going to promote your 'pay-what-you-can' night to university students, then don't offer the same group 'Two-for-the-price-of-one' tickets on competing nights.

- Take care to make those who receive offers feel they are being targeted personally, and not part of a scattergun approach. If someone books tickets on the basis of an offer and then receives a better offer when you are desperately trying to fill a house, they will, understandably, be unimpressed.

- Keep types of offers to a minimum. If you are working through a venue's box office, too many 'buyer-types' will only confuse staff. Box office staff should be able to identify the authenticity of an offer within seconds. You don't need more than two or three types of deals. If you are planning have a 'pay-what-you-can' night, consider this one of your 'deals'.

- Avoid panic-papering and panic-discounting *wherever possible.* The least effective deals occur when houses are low and companies put out heaps of offers at the last minute. Sometimes even mainstream companies do this if tickets aren't moving, but flooding the market with heavily discounted tickets smacks of desperation—it gives the impression that the show is a dud. If potential buyers (or industry) perceive this, you may not even be able to give tickets away.
- Ensure deals don't cost you too much. Save discounts for traditionally slow or hard-to-sell nights. Restrict tickets to sponsors to a range of nights (say, Tuesday–Thursday). Ditto for media giveaways.

Supporter discounts

The early bird catches the worm. Dangle the worm early to make it look tasty enough (and not like leftovers!) for your special supporters. Send out your offers via snailmail or email as soon as your promotional material is ready (three to four weeks out from opening).

Early-bird deals generally offer a special deal for the first few shows of the season. The best targets for this deal are people who know the company or who have supported you in the past, and the discount should be substantial enough to make them feel like a special friend. If your company has already mounted a few shows, use the names you have captured through box office systems or via guest books; this ever-expanding list is great for early-bird incentives. And remember that these people are potential subscribers, should you ever be in a position to develop packages.

Think of doing a 'two-for-the-price-of-one' special (on adult ticket prices) for this group, or price them at least $4 or $5 below the concession rate. If you are doing a direct mail-out, include a personalised letter and thank them for their previous support (see Chapter 5 for more details). If you're strapped for cash and time, simply put a 'slash sticker' with the offer details on it across your postcard and mail them without envelopes. If you have the money and your list is big, you could consider printing a special flyer. Printing these at the same time as opening night invitations may make it more affordable. You can send early-bird specials via email, but if you can afford direct mail, it's a more 'personal' method of delivery to a special list of supporters.

Don't be shy about recruiting friends to spruik tickets for you. Consider offering a double pass here and there to mates with extensive email networks who will actively spread the word. Or offer personal incentives over and above ticket discounts (a bottle of sparkling, free programs) if they organise a group booking. Run a competition (with a nice prize) to the cast or crew member who brings in the most patrons!

An extra word here about family and general 'friends'. There is nothing wrong with offering a great deal to loved ones, but bear in mind that those who are personally close to you are generally the most eager patrons. Parents, siblings and cashed-up mates (from other industries!) won't baulk at buying a ticket, and will be keen to support you any way they can. As mercenary as it sounds, don't be shy about letting loved ones pay full price, or allowing them to talk well-heeled mates into doing likewise. But do encourage them to come along early!

Other in-season deals

The greater your networks (whether personal or developed by the company), or your access to networks attached to season hubs, the more you can target ticket offers to people who will be *specifically* interested in your production. Try and get to these groups early and think of them as your second-wave attack; keep significant discounts to small groups of loyal supporters and offer more modest incentives to wider networks.

For example, plug your 'industry rate' or 'industry night' to appropriate networks, such as the staff of major performing arts companies, institutions and galleries, the membership of bodies such as ANPC, AWG, Playworks, Musica Viva and MEAA, and other organisations that specifically service your state or territory. If your show has a strong nod to another artform such as visual arts, literature or music, then make sure you look beyond theatre industry circles. The earlier you circulate information to such organisations, the more likely they can plug your show and advertise a special rate through their email networks and newsletters. It's fairly easy to identify these bodies through the web; follow the links from your state or territory arts funding body and Ozco websites.

If the season hub you are working in has an email database of patrons from their previous show, offer a ticket deal slightly below concession rate for one or two specific performances. Do this at least two weeks before you open. Performing arts and literature students are great for previews, offer them comps or cheap tickets. Research specific student or staff contacts for courses if the play (or playwright) is on a university reading list, and plug your concession rate or perhaps offer a cheaper rate for traditionally less-patronised performances ('Super Student Sunday Special—$18').

If you have a sponsor with good corporate networks, ask them to distribute information about your show and *endorse* it through any newsletters or staff e-bulletins (give yourselves plenty of lead time here). Corporate citizens are generally more cashed-up, so a general plug may be all that's needed. If discounts are part of your sponsor deal, then offer concession rates to staff.

Media giveaways, particularly for street press and community radio are great for keeping publicity on the boil throughout the season. Your publicist should control how they are distributed; a double pass here and there is usually enough incentive to ensure media plugs. Specify performances that tickets can be used for.

Group and school bookings

Group booking schemes will not work for every indie show, particularly if it's very offbeat or 'off the beaten track' venue-wise, but they are great when there's a large identifiable group with a special interest in your show. They are also a terrific way for well-connected members of your group (those who know lots of lawyers, bankers or office workers for instance) to sell the show to cashed-up groups who will enjoy it.

Spend a bit of time researching the target group, then offer information, photos and your group booking rate for dissemination in staff newsletters and e-letters. If the show is about hairdressers, offer a group booking rate to local hairdressing businesses, for example, and for distribution through industry networks such as unions or representing bodies. If the show has a cult literary bent (a dramatisation of the life of Sylvia Plath, Virginia Woolf or Sir Arthur Conan Doyle), target adult writing courses. Draft specific copy for each sector that can be used for personalised letters and releases. The pitches work best with shows that have broad appeal and a friendly 'hook'. A fun night out for a group is more likely to be snapped up.

The great benefit of group bookings is that you don't sacrifice too much income (ticket prices should be between concession and full rates), and they can be slotted anywhere in the season. There are a couple of rules: give yourself a few months lead-time for research and implementation. Don't 'undersell' your product—a good group booking rate is discount enough. Enhance it, if you must, by developing packages such as a 'dinner and show' deal with a local restaurant or, if you are running your own bar, use an alcohol or catering sponsorship to offer a free drink and some nibblies to early group bookings. Bear in mind that these endeavours are time-consuming and somebody will need to manage the whole process.

Most importantly, don't waste time pitching an 'inappropriate' show to the corporate sector and don't fib about your show! Be honest with yourself about its appeal to a particular group and the nature of your production. If you pitch a show about online dating with lots of vibrant images, when it's really a dark journey into the mind of a serial killer (who goes on an internet date in one scene), you are asking for trouble. Be honest about any nudity, graphic sexual images, violence or highly colourful language. Thirty annoyed customers at the end of the night may bring in a few dollars but it won't garner a new group of supporters that you can target again for your next (suitable) show, a far more important aim.

This final rule is especially important for school bookings. Companies dedicated to performing syllabus plays or who deliberately hit key learning areas with their productions can attract strong box-office, and there are producers dedicated to selling (Department of Education approved) work. It's a fairly specialist area and I won't spend much time discussing it here.

Briefly, though, if you think your show is suitable for school students, it's certainly worth comparing the subject matter and form of your work with units of secondary school study. Talk to the Department of Education in your state or territory or ask teacher friends and colleagues. Productions of classics, absurd works, physical and culturally-specific theatre and some new Australian work may well attract interest from secondary schools. If your season hub or venue has an Education Officer or a database of school contacts, look into the possibility of setting up special performances for students. I've seen many companies get matinees up by targeting their old schools or contacts they've made through teaching and workshop gigs. Again, you need to be up-front about any bad language, nudity or controversial subject matter (abortion and euthanasia for instance), particularly if you are not offering teacher's notes. If you don't know what ages are suitable for your show, then recommend enquiring teachers read the play. Once again, to set this up properly long lead times are required. Teachers need time to make decisions (arts teachers are often inundated with glossy flyers) and get approval for outings. You may also be hampered by exam times or conflicts with a busy extra-curricular period.

Emergency tactics

If everything you've planned (or, let's face it, *not* planned) goes awry and you are faced with poor sales and dismal houses, your only choice may be to get those offers out there. If this is the case, avoid using lists you've already offered deals, and be wary of fatiguing your contacts with reminders. It's good to have a couple of fresh options up your sleeve for emergencies, so when you're plotting targets, keep one or two in reserve. Deluging the same people with new and lower offers will only confuse and annoy them, particularly if they've already paid for their tickets.

Complimentary tickets

Devise a clear comp system at the start that specifies what *types* of comps are allowed and *who* is authorised to allocate them. Choose one member of your team, preferably the producer, to be your card-carrying 'Complimentary Ticket Monitor' (CTM). Make sure they have a stern attitude and a big stick, because nothing can whittle away a co-op's earnings more than rampant 'comp pillaging'. This person should also be responsible for accepting (or rejecting) comp requests from the rest of the company, and they should book them in through the box office whether you are taking your own bookings or working through a venue's system. Under no circumstances should cast and crew be permitted to book ad-hoc comps individually. This practice will defeat any chance you have of tracking comps and will consume potential profit! Another reason to keep a tight rein on comps is that many venues will limit how many you can have free of ticket handling fees.

A basic system is outlined here:

- **Media comps:** controlled by your publicist and CTM. These are 'priority' comps; make sure these requests are responded to quickly and booked in correctly.
- **Promotional comps (as discussed above in 'deals and discounts'):** devised and controlled by the CTM and, where appropriate, the Season Hub Manager, and managed by the Box Office Manager.
- **VIP comps (casting directors, VIP industry):** strictly controlled by the CTM. Cast and crew make requests to the CTM, so that they can be checked for authenticity.
- **Personal comps (for family and friends):** one or two tickets per cast or crew member for opening night, the same for closing night and two tickets in-season. Booked in by the CTM.

Working with box office

Most established indie venues offer a booking service and may contractually insist that you use it. They charge a handling fee per ticket sold, and may also charge for ticket stock. Standard credit card booking fees should be passed on to the customer at the time of booking.

A professional box-office system, even a simply-structured one, is well worth these costs. Imagine the work involved in taking bookings, recording them correctly according to ticket-type, setting up cash systems, issuing tickets, keeping track of deals, reconciling income and preparing reports. What about unforeseen circumstances? If you have ever had to cancel a performance due to illness, you will know how much work is involved. If you are in a basic venue and have to manage the box office yourselves, find team members to staff the desk each night with experience of handling cash *and* people;

someone with retail experience is ideal. If you recruit a family member with these skills, you can be sure they'll be careful with your money and tough about freebies! If they are taking phone bookings for you, make sure that they have all relevant information by the phone, including information about parking and venue accessibility.

When you have signed your venue contract, make an appointment with the Box Office Manager (BOM) or primary ticket sales contact. Ask them to talk you through box office procedure, so that you clearly understand how it works. Once you are properly contracted, the BOM should 'build' your show into their ticketing system. Make sure you know the exact date your tickets will be released for sale.

There are a number of things you can do to make the company's relationship with box office a happy one:

- Most venues will give you information forms to fill out. Make sure box office staff have full and accurate details of your show title and company name (for ticket printing), and *all* ticket prices. You also need to specify acceptable concessions. Inform the staff of the show running time and if there is an interval.

- Provide a clear and lively one–to–two paragraph description of your show, including the names of cast and creatives. Box office staff can refer to this when patrons ask about the show.

- Let the BOM know if you wish to hold a certain number of 'house seats' (reserved seats for VIPs and emergencies) for each performance and if any seats *cannot* be sold due to sightline or safety issues.

- Is there nudity, intense bad-language or culturally offensive practices in the production? Are there gunshots, smoking or strobe effects? The box office must know the answers to these questions *before* they start selling tickets. Many adult patrons enquire about tickets for children—identify a suitable age threshold for the show.

- Provide the BOM with a full company contact list.

- Discuss your company's complimentary ticket agreement. Nominate *one* person to book in comps, and instruct box office staff to only take such bookings from that person. Always make your requests in writing (fax or email) and give box office staff 24 hours notice wherever possible.
- Managing a raft of deals and details can be confusing, especially if the box office has a lot of casual staff. They may not be able to build them all into the system at the same time; explain the deals in writing as they are created and give the box office time to set them up. Do not send out offers *before* the box office hears about them! If you keep your deals to two or three 'buyer-types', as I've already suggested, it will be easier for box office to track and implement them.
- If you want to know which groups respond to your offers, ask the box office if they can code them. Even if you target several groups with the same offer, you can ask each group to quote something identifiable to box office when they book (eg the Sydney Uni Sunday Special) to get a rough breakdown of respondents.
- Sometimes you have to arrange group bookings before tickets officially go on sale. It is not ideal, but if it happens, brief the BOM clearly, so that the transfer to system bookings goes smoothly. If the box office is responsible for ticketing the show, then you should pass on all information, including individual patron names and contacts and any collected money as soon as possible.
- Ask if there is a ticket exchange or refund policy in place.
- Discuss how preview and opening night systems work. Identify how many seats you would like taken off sale for preview and opening performances to accommodate invited guests. This may not happen automatically, so organise it early! If you are taking your own preview and opening night RSVPs, prepare alphabetised

RSVP lists, so that you can simply 'tick off' guests as they respond. Then provide the box office staff with your final, *accurate*, *typed* and *alphabetised* guest lists the day before. Hand-written lists with crossed-out scrawls will make life hell for box office staff distributing tickets on the night, and any dressing down you get as a result will be deserved!

- Let box office know if they will be responsible for selling programs or merchandise. Also advise them if programs will be given out free to preview and/or opening night guests.

- Check in with box office each day regarding daily sales. Your BOM should provide you with a sales report at least every couple of days and a weekly reconciliation report. If you don't know how to read them, ask. Most systems provide lots of useful data about sales trends that you'll want to take note of.

- Make sure you cordially invite box office (and venue) staff to attend your show. The earlier they come, the more knowledge they have of your show when they are selling it to patrons!

Finally, make your whole company aware that selling the show is one of the few activities that lasts through the life of a production; from signing a venue contract to the final performance. 'Selling out' is a rare phenomenon, and if you are lucky enough to do it, it usually doesn't happen until late in the season, so keep that ball moving until you kick the final goal!

9

Setting up house

Things that go bump in the theatre

You've signed the lease and the keys are jingling in your pocket—it's time to move into the house! Taking possession of the theatre is a genuinely exciting moment, but, as with other parts of the game, the secret is in the planning. Production week is one of the most time-critical periods in the whole process. If you are not *meticulously* prepared for the deluge of tasks the company is about to face (along with all the unexpected curve balls), then be prepared to witness excitement turn to chaos. There is nothing more debilitating for a company, which has performed solidly in the practice runs, to find itself tripping over an unfinished set.

Chapter 4 lists a few crewing scenarios that may be of use to personnel-challenged companies, but if you are really serious about minimising production dramas you need a production manager. This person will be responsible for venue inspections, scheduling bump-in and out, organising show risk assessments and licences, liaising with designers, stage managers and the producer regarding set and costume budgets and builds, and generally making sure that the whole thing comes together in production week and is taken apart properly during bump-out. They need basic knowledge of technical equipment and how to interpret plans, and should be pretty handy with a hammer and drill. In many ways the production manager is the star 'producer' of production week; the better skilled and organised they are, the more it will free up the overall producer for marketing and promotional tasks.

In order to make sure that production week and bump-out are a success, the producer should maintain regular contact with the production manager and check they have the following tasks under control. If you don't have a production manager then you may need to distribute these tasks among the group:

● Once a hire contract has been signed, the venue should supply all relevant technical specifications, including theatre floor plans, a lighting grid plan and equipment lists. Make time to visit the venue as soon as possible and chat with its technical manager. If it's an older venue, run a tape measure over it for accuracy (rough theatre spaces are rarely measured the same way twice!) and check out loading areas, particularly the doors. A common mistake is ensuring the set will fit the space without checking if pieces will actually fit through loading doorways. Don't assume a piece of equipment is working just because it is listed, or that you can drill anywhere and paint over everything. If you are using video media, make sure that you are able to achieve what you have planned; investigate the rigging points and projection distances required for any video equipment. Not all theatres have or provide access to prop, set and costumes stores, but it's worth asking if they do.

● If the show involves anything that may require licences or special permission, then raise this early with the venue's technical liaison. This includes any weight-bearing rigging, use of liquid on the stage floor or walls (such as mud or rain), fire, firearms or special effects. Better to be told 'no' early than to arrive at the venue with no alternative solution to a critical effect.

Humphrey Bower and Sophia Hall in last seen imagining's production of *The Reader* for The Blue Room. Photo: Ashley de Prazer.

- The production manager should undertake a risk assessment study for the show. This is now a legal requirement in most states, so if you are not sure how to do it ask the venue's Occupational Health and Safety Committee or Officer for help. Basically, a simple set of procedures will help you to identify potentially risky or unsafe practices so that you can assess, and then eliminate or reduce, the risk to performers, crew and audience. A risk assessment may lead you to identify trip hazards on set, lighting states that reduce visibility for actors to an unsafe level, or costumes that need to be fire-proofed. Information can be found on each state's Workcover website **[W19]**. The Australia Council has a booklet detailing a five-step risk management process for organisations which is an informative introduction to the topic, even if you are just mounting one-off seasons here and there.

- You may find that licences or certificates are required for some of your activities; the most common of these are for the use of naked flame onstage, weight-bearing rigging and replica weapons (replica weapons cannot be left unattended at any time backstage and must be locked up between performances). Any licences required should be pursued as early as possible.

- A word here about smoking in performance. The long arm of the law hasn't yet reached our stages, but the prospect of a legal ban on stage smoking isn't too hard to envisage. Meanwhile, small venues without decent ventilation often come under fire from patrons who don't take kindly to being smoked-out by performers. Even in larger theatres, most patrons, asthmatic or otherwise, prefer smoke-free performances. My advice is to eliminate smoking from your production wherever possible (an actor deciding that their character *would* smoke is not sufficient reason). If the text is explicit, and it would undermine the sense of things not to smoke, then execute it in a controlled way. The repeated action of lighting a low gram cigarette and puffing once or twice before extinguishing it, can give a pretty solid impression of chain-smoking. Try smoking as far upstage as possible, and don't let cigarettes burn away on floors or in ashtrays. Cigars are a no-no, unless you want to clear the theatre faster than a bad comedian.

- Patrons should be informed of any stage smoking at point of sale, but signage at the theatre is also important. This also applies to any other smoke, and to strobe effects, nudity and excessively bad language.

- Draft a schedule for production week. This should include *everything* that needs to happen during the week: the delivery of set items and materials; construction, painting and sealing (make sure you allow adequate time for paint to dry); the rigging, focusing and plotting of lights; sound and video plots; production photos, on-stage rehearsal, through to technical and dress rehearsals and your first performance. Make sure that designers have all materials ready for technical rehearsals (tracks burned to disc, edited footage prepared for use) and schedule time for technical 'fix-ups'.

● Bump-out should also be planned, including set and costume storage, returns and disposal, cleaning of dressing rooms, and the return of the theatre to its original state (including painting and plugging of holes and damage repair). You should aim to complete this within the allotted timeframe—venue managements get very angry when companies haven't organised transport to remove *everything* in time for the next hirer's bump-in. If you need a truck for set delivery and removal, book this early, particularly if you don't want to pay through the nose for it.

● If the venue supplies a technical manager to assist with your bump-in then, in the timeframe they request, supply them with:
    ● set and lighting plans
    ● a clean, complete and up-to-date copy of the script
    ● technical notes, including a lighting and sound synopsis
    ● bump-in and bump-out schedules (see Schedule 9, page 174)
    ● a company contact list

● If the venue supplies a sound and lighting operator, send them a copy of the rehearsal schedule and invite them to a full run of the show in the final rehearsal week.

Most indie companies don't supply nearly enough 'bodies' to help them bump-in and out. Don't be shy of asking friends or family members who are good with a hammer and saw to pitch in, even for a few hours. When it comes to painting, nailing and sanding, many hands make light work, and give actors more time to acclimatise to their new working environment.

A sneak peek

Whilst your production team is whipping up a storm in the theatre, the producer will be firming up preview and opening night houses.

One preview means you have only one chance for the cast and crew to do a 'live test' before throwing back the veil for serious industry on opening night. We've already suggested that sponsors or students are good audiences for previews. Try to maintain as relaxed an atmosphere as you can. Things can and do go wrong on preview night—audiences half expect it, so don't get too strung out if something falls off the wall or a lighting state goes awry. The director and designer will be taking notes and thanking their lucky stars that it happened then and not on opening night! If you feel that things are really dodgy (especially if you haven't yet done a full, uninterrupted dress rehearsal), it's perfectly acceptable for the director to say a few words before the show, to rally the audience by appealing to their sense of adventure for an unpredictable ride—but check the venue or season hub's policy on this. A house of five or ten people doesn't really help actors prepare for the shift to high-octane performance levels, so do your best to fill the house. The closer you can simulate opening night conditions, the more relaxed and confident your performers will be for that hardcore industry crowd.

Previews are very useful for garnering comment, so invite a couple of peers or trusted colleagues along to give you some feedback. You could also ask preview audiences to complete a questionnaire (a fair exchange for free tickets), if you wish to get a more expansive response.

Your production manager will have scheduled times for technical corrections, but it's also common for directors to schedule artistic fix-ups for the day of opening. Make 'calls' as late in the day as possible, giving the company time to rest adequately beforehand and to eat and prepare in a relaxed manner in the hours leading up to performance.

SCHEDULE 9: Bump-in Schedule for *Half & Half* (The Chess Club)

DATE	TIME	JOB DESCRIPTION	REQUIRED
Sunday 29 August	6.30pm	*Four on the Floor* finishes	
	7.45pm	*Four in the Floor* bump out	
	8pm	Bump in flats	GD, H x 4
	8pm	Drill attachments for cupboard	GD, BB
	8pm	Start painting walls	PR, H x 10, LL, SH, TM, MC
	8pm	Lighting pre-rig	LP, AJ
	10.30pm	Paint floor	LL, PR, SH
	11pm	Finish	
Monday 30 August	9am–12pm	Finish rigging lighting and flash	LP, AJ
(Lee not	9am–1pm	Bump in soil, mound, astroturf	GD, PR, BB
available from	9am–1pm	Bump in cupboards and screen	GD, BB
9am–1pm)	9am–1pm	Rig water system	GD
	9am–1pm	Bump in costumes	AB, PR
	9am–1pm	Rig false roof points	GS, BB, MC
	12pm	LUNCH FOR LX CREW	
	1pm–5pm	Lighting focus	LP, AJ
	5pm	DINNER	
	5pm	Rig false roof	GS, BB, MC
	7pm–11pm	Plotting	LL, LP, AJ, MC, TM, AB
	8pm–11pm	Painting touch-ups/second coat and aquatech floor	LL, SH

DATE	TIME	JOB DESCRIPTION	REQUIRED
Tuesday 31 August	9am–10.30am	Tech time	TBC
	10.30am	Fire test with Sydney Council representative	TM, SH, LL
	11am	EARLY LUNCH	
	12pm	Technical rehearsal	ALL
	5pm	DINNER	
	6pm	Continue technical rehearsal	ALL
	11pm	Finish	
Wednesday 1 September	9am–1pm	Tech time/Rehearsals on stage	TBC
	1pm–2pm	LUNCH	
	1.25pm	1/2 hour call	
	2pm	Dress rehearsal # 1 (photos)	ALL
	6pm	DINNER	
	7.40pm	1/2 hour call	
	8.15pm	Preview	ALL
Thursday 2 September	9am–1pm	Tech time	TBC
	1pm–2pm	LUNCH	
	3pm–5pm	Rehearsals on stage	LL, MC, TM
	3.30pm	*Getaway filming rehearsals in theatre*	LL, MC, TM, SH
	5pm–6pm	DINNER	
	7.40pm	1/2 hour call	
	8.15pm	Opening night	ALL

LL: Lee Lewis, director; **LP**: Luiz Pampolha, lighting designer; **AB**: Alice Babidge, costume designer; **BB**: Brett Boardman, executive producer; **SH**: Sam Hawker, producer; **GD**: Greg Dalton, production manager; **PR**: Pier Rudd, stage manager; **MC**: Mark Constable, cast; **TM**: Tim Morgan, cast; **AJ**: Allison Jeny, technical manager; **H**: Helpers x 10. Prepared by Sam Hawker.

Setting up opening night

Before you don your best party frock or suit, let's travel back in time a few weeks. How did all these smiling, chattering guests get to be milling happily in your foyer?

Opening night is most likely to be a fully invited house, and your guests may include industry (artistic directors, directors, producers, actors), reviewers and other media, company supporters and friends, guests of cast and crew and VIP guests including funding committee members, politicians, sponsors and celebrities. Putting together an opening night list is a tricky thing. It's a night to launch the project before your peers and other industry members, to share and celebrate your artistic achievements with friends and family, to promote the company to funding bodies and other potential supporters, and to invite media to comment and project your show's appeal to the general public. That's a huge undertaking for one evening. No wonder it generates such a lot of nervous energy!

You may not be trying to do all these things. It's important for each company to ascertain its own goals and invite accordingly, rather than sending invitations to every address it has. If you're a student group with limited experience, it may not be helpful to subject yourself to a major paper's blowtorch reviewer, and funding committee members may benefit more from seeing your work at a later stage in the company's development. If you're a new director and you feel this work hasn't come together well, then perhaps it's unwise to hound mainstream artistic directors into seeing the show. A rising indie company, however, with a couple of decent shows under its belt and the confidence to match, should go for it!

Media will always be a priority for opening night, and it's wise to 'set aside' an allocation of tickets, so that you don't get caught short if other guests RSVP quickly. If your publicist is taking media RSVPs, check numbers regularly.

If you are dipping into every sector, it's wise to balance VIPs with some friendly faces. Every seat on opening night should be doing the company some good, whether it be taken by a reviewer or a supportive colleague who will laugh (when it's appropriate) and give out a supportive vibe. An opening night audience consisting entirely of 'arms folded' industry practitioners can be a nightmare for the cast, particularly in a small venue where eyeballing is unavoidable. The mix of guests should contribute to a positive experience. Another way of diversifying the audience, is to invite 'opinion leaders' from other business sectors, not just the entertainment industry. If your show is perfect for a particular type of patron, then invite opinion leaders for this target audience. Consider social club organisers, local business people such as lawyers, hairdressers and cab drivers (quite a few go to the theatre!).

VIP Invitations to indie shows should land in letterboxes two to three weeks out from the first day of bump-in. Media invitations should go out a week or two before this. Some small companies get general invitations out a month or six weeks ahead, but this doesn't stop guests cancelling when a bigger and better invitation lands on their desk a week later. It's also easy for people to lose invitations when they have too many weeks to RSVP.

Reviews

Reviewers can be strange and enigmatic beasts; some are affable, easy to contact and forthcoming with their views, others prefer less personal contact. Many radio stations and publications only have one reviewer, but for major newspapers there may be several and arts editors will allocate reviewers for specific events. You should send media invitations to the arts editor and all the reviewers for the paper, so they are aware of the show and can request to review it if they wish. It is sometimes possible to gently shape proceedings by following up your invitation to your preferred reviewer and giving *them* the opportunity to make this request. It doesn't of course guarantee they will be allocated. This is always delicate work, and best not attempted if you're not light on your feet. Nothing gets an editor's nose out of joint more than a demand for a particular reviewer for your show.

Whilst some reviewers are happy to have a beer and a chat in the foyer after the show, most prefer to slip away without engaging in conversation. This doesn't mean they didn't like your show. You should *never* contact a reviewer between the opening and when the review appears. The timing of a review going to print generally rests with arts editors. Sometimes even though reviewers attend opening nights, the review takes forever to appear, or never appears. This generally reflects space restrictions, but occasionally a reviewer will spare a small company if they don't feel they can write anything positive about the show.

Reviews are a historical record of the show's existence and can be very useful when compiling theatrical archives for your company or yourself. However, while they may have an impact on your show's box office, they are not a substitute for good publicity. Too many indie companies rely on reviews to get the word out to audiences, but if the word isn't good, or it is too late, the strategy will backfire.

Nothing delights a company more than a rave review and nothing crushes its spirit more than a stinker. Review-rage is right up there with road-rage; it will raise your blood pressure and cause you to do and say things you wouldn't normally dream of, but this achieves nothing in terms of your development. Theatre reviews are less formal (and useful) evaluations of artistic enterprise than they were in days of old. Increasingly, they read more like personal opinion pieces than useful critiques for artists and audiences. So don't take a review too personally, treat it as one person's opinion with which you can choose to agree or disagree. And don't ever abuse a critic; he or she is only doing the job you invited them to do. If the review is intolerably cruel, abusive or seriously factually inaccurate, then a letter to the arts editor is justified, but in twenty years of practice, I have only ever seen this right actioned two or three times. My advice is that you enjoy the positive reviews with good grace, take the bad ones on the chin, and actively invite feedback from the evaluators who really count—your trusted colleagues, mentors and audience.

Invitations and RSVPs

If you have a great printing deal that allows you to produce a beautiful invitation, that's a bonus, but fancy cards are not necessary. A laser printer or commercial photocopier can produce a neatly printed invitation with clear details which, accompanied by a show flyer or postcard and, for media, a press release, is all you need. It sounds obvious but make sure that you include the show title, the company and writer's name, venue address details and opening night date and time. Check that the day of the week matches the date; this is a common mistake and is very confusing for guests. Include an RSVP date (five to seven days before opening is good), phone number and/ or email address. If your show starts at 8pm, list it as 7.45pm; the curtain is more likely to go up on time if guests are encouraged to pick up their tickets and have a drink a bit earlier, and it gives box office staff a chance to ticket any wait-listed guests more efficiently. If you don't want guest tickets to be passed onto a third party, or to be used on any other night, then make the invitation 'non-transferable'. Whatever you decide about transfers, make sure you tell box office early (put it in writing), so they know how to deal with requests. If you only wish to receive acceptances then indicate this; RSVP (respondez s'il vous plait) means 'respond please', which invites people to accept *or* decline. When your template is complete, have someone else check for accuracy and any omissions.

Ensure that whoever is taking RSVPs, be it the venue's box office, the publicist, the producer or company representative, keeps an accurate written list of respondents and a daily tally. If media RSVPs are being handled separately, compare these tallies regularly. There is no need to notify receipt of RSVPs, unless you are fully booked. Even big companies rarely 'close off' at house capacity; overbooking to compensate for last minute cancellations and 'no shows' is very common. Juggling RSVP demands for a small venue can sometimes feel like a high wire act. It's not out of the question to lose 20% of your house in the hours before opening during 'flu season or in bad weather, and there is no contingency if absolutely everyone turns up. Box Office Managers should have a good idea of the 'trend' at their venue. 10% above capacity is about average for overbooking.

Big jumps in acceptances often occur close to performance, so tally regularly in the few days before opening to avoid an unmanageable overbook. If you do find yourself in a sticky situation, you may have to transfer company comps (or understanding friends) to another performance. There will always be a couple of people who turn up on opening night swearing that they've RSVP'd, even though you have no record of it. Media should never be refused, and depending on the VIP status of the guest (yes, this is highly elitist and unforgivably 'un-PC', I know), admit them without argument, or ask them to wait until other guests have collected their tickets. It's not worth challenging people in a big way unless you have accepted all RSVPs personally and verbally, as the mistake could very well be yours!

A handful of people really must have tickets for opening night no matter how late they RSVP. Make sure you leave room for reviewers and sponsors who are likely to attend. Sponsors are often tardy, particularly if they are not really theatre-goers. Contact them before you're booked up to check if they will be using their tickets. It's extremely rude for guests to RSVP and fail to attend without calling to cancel—a call even an hour before the show is acceptable and helpful to box office. Season hubs often keep a list of repeat offenders and drop them from their lists, a practice you may wish to adopt if you are mounting several shows a year. If you receive invitations yourself, it makes sense to practise the same level of consideration as you expect from others.

Whoever handles RSVPs will also be responsible for preparing final guest lists. Prepare two typed lists (one for media and one for other guests), in alphabetical order and use a font size that lets you find names quickly. Give these to box office the day before opening and provide updated lists on the day of opening, if necessary.

It's perfectly reasonable to limit guest tickets to opening night, but you should allow transfers if you really want someone to see your work. If a general guest can't make opening night, offer to transfer them into the first couple of shows, so that you can keep comps down later in the season when you expect more paying customers. It's a goodwill gesture you could extend to people who RSVP after you've closed off. Also try to accommodate artistic directors and professional producers who are often inundated with invitations, so they can come on a night they have a gap in their diaries.

When a lot of shows open on the same night, a reviewer unable to attend yours might request seats for another night during the first week. This is a perfectly acceptable practice. In an increasingly competitive environment, it's becoming common for indie shows, even in season hubs, to go unreviewed by major newspapers; but if the editor has not categorically stated that they will not send a reviewer, continue to push a few days after opening.

If other media guests ask to transfer to a performance early in the season, it's polite to accommodate them, but don't feel obliged to pander to unreasonable requests. Make an effort to keep people happy if you are interested in developing or maintaining relationships with them. A hired publicist will automatically handle these requests and if the ask isn't distinctly advantageous to the company (say your show is sold out and a journalist wants to come in the last week), then they'll probably chat to you about it. But remember that professional publicists are usually juggling several shows at once, and need to keep their contacts happy for the good of all the clients they are servicing now and in the future.

Media and schmoozing

You or your publicist will need to prepare media kits for opening night. If you've already sent out a lot of information, you can keep these simple; a little folder with a media release, theatre program, CD-ROM with a few production shots and a card or contact details should suffice. If you don't have enough money to supply discs to everyone, then one or two of your best shots can be emailed on the day of your opening. Whilst box office is ticketing VIP guests, publicists traditionally greet media separately at a small table, and personally hand them tickets and a media kit. This courtesy also enables reviewers (who are working that night as well!) to collect tickets quickly and relax in the foyer with other industry members.

It's important for the producer to do a little schmoozing on opening night. This doesn't mean interrogating everyone about their response (if you ask what guests think on opening night, don't be surprised if they're honest. Reviewers will be very unimpressed if you quiz them). Apart from liaising with box office staff regarding ticket allocations and dealing with any crisis, it's the producer's job to welcome guests, invite them to stick around for a drink after the show and make introductions where appropriate.

Programs and foyer boards

Regular indie patrons (and media) are used to low-budget show programs, but that's no excuse for a really sloppy job—it reeks of last-minute preparation. Photocopied programs are absolutely fine, but make some effort to include information that isn't just a rehash of your flyer copy and media release.

Hunt and gather as early as you can—not during production week when your creative team is flat out. You should include relevant information about the company and production, credits and biographies for all cast, crew and affiliated workers. Write a company history and include supporting quotes and testimonials. Production and play notes also make for interesting reading. A section for 'thankyous' and any necessary sponsor or funding acknowledgment is a must—don't forget logos and any credits or notes that season hubs or venues may require.

You can re-use the biographical paragraphs you needed for publicity in the program, but if you want a different feel, ask each cast member to write something more casual during the first week of rehearsal. Eschew Monty Pythonesque comedy biogs unless they're really appropriate to the show and *everyone* agrees to make fun of themselves. If one biog reads like the 'dead parrot sketch' and everyone else's is neat and professional, the company will look ... well, rather silly. Hopefully the director will be lucid enough to supply a few hundred words of production notes, but if they resist, collate some interesting facts about the writer and the history of the play, particularly if it is a classic or it has specific cultural or social interest. If you are quoting from printed material, obtain any necessary formal permission. If your program is of the coverless photocopy variety, you will probably make more money asking for a gold coin donation rather than by trying to sell it. If it's just a one page job with a cast list, you really should give it away.

If you have the funds to produce a professionally printed program, or better still, procure a printing sponsor, and the content is informative and interesting, you'll be able to charge patrons a few dollars for it. You can also include photographs and sell 'advertising space'. An ad in a polished program can be exchanged for valuable contra (such as opening night alcohol or catering).

Most theatres have foyer boards for cast and crew photos, articles and reviews. The producer should gather material for this during rehearsals; a half empty board on opening night looks sad and unprofessional. If only some of your actors have proper headshots, then consider doing an informal photo shoot with a digital camera or something fun and quirky. Quite a few B Sharp shows have taken impromptu polaroids of their company during production week— it's cheap and quick, but the style of everyone's photo is consistent and they look surprisingly good on the boards. Make sure you attach names to faces! Fill the rest of the board with production photos, press articles and, later, any positive reviews. Aim to have the board looking good for preview night.

Catering

It isn't necessary to spend a great deal of money on your opening night function, but if you can afford it, a glass of bubbly and a couple of cheese plates will help to keep guests around for post-show chatting and celebration. The success of an opening night has often been gauged by how long guests stick around; the later the bar closes, the better the show has generally been received!

If your venue does not have any sponsorship or catering restrictions, you should attempt to procure a case of sponsored sparkling wine (from a distributor or your friendly local vendor in exchange for an ad in the program) for your opening night function. If your guest list (and program) is particularly attractive, it's also worth pitching to a local restaurant or cafe for sponsored food platters. If catering is going to be a do-it-yourself job, make sure that you keep things as simple as your venue's facilities; without an oven or adequate bench space, there's no point in contemplating hot snacks or food that requires elaborate on-site construction. If there is no refrigeration, don't serve salmon mousse.

You may have to use the venue's resident caterer, which can be prohibitively expensive. If you have no money for catering, ask if you can supply your own chips and dips. Some venues will make allowances for unfunded ventures—it doesn't hurt to ask. If you do get permission, make sure that you clean up at the end of the night.

It's most likely that you'll need to purchase alcohol from the venue's bar. If you're strapped for cash then buy enough sparkling wine to cover half to three quarters of your guest numbers (not everyone will indulge) for a single glass (you'll get about 6 glasses out of a bottle) and run a small tab for soft drinks or juice. Guests can pay for any other drinks. If you have, say, $400 or more to spend, then put a set amount of money on the bar, and specify what drinks it will cover (sparkling, house white and red, standard beer and soft drink). Once that runs out, guests can purchase additional drinks. If there is a lot of free alcohol available, then it's only responsible to supply some decent food to help soak it up. If you have enough alcohol to offer guests a drink on arriving, it can help to cajole people into a more receptive mood.

On with the show

Opening a show is like having a baby; once it's delivered, the hormones (adrenalin!) that have been keeping everyone pumped, suddenly head for someone else's rehearsal room! The 'second night blues' can hit even the most hard-working casts.

As a producer you can help by making sure early houses are solidly booked. The come-down from opening night can be really hard for co-ops if the house drops overnight from 100 to 15; so do your pre-sales work (as outlined in Chapter 8), to avoid a morale nosedive. You're also likely to be entertaining media, including reviewers, for your first three or four shows; make sure the cast realise this.

The 'dynamic' or 'personality' of a company is unique to each show. Just because a show isn't doing well, doesn't necessarily mean morale will falter. I have witnessed casts grow stronger together and retain a wonderful sense of professionalism through rotten reviews and poor houses and, conversely, I have also seen cast relations and decent behaviour plummet during sell-out seasons.

Unless you have worked together a few times, it's hard to know how a company is going to handle three or four weeks sharing a damp and smelly cupboard-sized dressing room. If people don't like each other, it's not ideal, but it should never affect the show. If it looks like bad blood will impact professionally, then the producer must keep an eye on the situation and if necessary intervene. Any seriously unprofessional behaviour, such as harassment or abuse or onstage sabotage should not be tolerated.

A producer who attends performances regularly will have their finger on the pulse of the company dynamic. Checking houses and monitoring sales reports are all part of a producer's job; but so are regular cast visits and issue debriefs, as they help to ensure the performing company is comfortable, happy and feels supported throughout the season.

⑩

Moving out and moving on

Documentation, remounts, touring, debriefing

The season is up and running and time has grown wings. You'll be planning a closing night party before you know it. Although it may feel like the project is coming to an end, a producer should be asking, 'is there a future for it elsewhere?'. Most indie companies are so stretched for time and money they rarely stop to consider that their hard labour has produced an asset that can be *maximised*. I have stressed the importance of good marketing images a number of times. Your second most important undertaking as producer is thorough documentation. Theatre is an ephemeral medium and once that curtain comes down, the only record of a show's existence (aside from memory) are documents collated from media sources or created by yourself.

Recording your history

It's crucial to video the show. Many companies don't do this, or not until their last performance, leaving no room for technical errors (the most common is that the tape runs out ten minutes before the end!). A good, clear video record of your show is not only hugely important for archival purposes, but can be used in support of funding and season-hub applications and for any re-mount or touring opportunities that arise. Companies always cite poverty as the reason for not videoing their show. But if you can't borrow a digital video camera from the venue or family and friends, it's possible to get a professional record of your show for $200 to $300. This is probably not much more than has been spent on paint, and in the long run, it's a more important investment. Try chatting to film and video schools, who may have students who want to gain practical experience.

If you are doing it yourself with a digital camera, shoot a run around mid-season (when the show is really firing) and at least one more. You'll learn from the first session the best angle and distance to shoot from, and it will give you a chance to learn how to frame certain scenes and correct sound levels.

The most important thing is that actors' faces and dialogue are *very clear*. No-one will bother to watch a tape full of distant, blobby heads or muffled voices overrun by a laughing audience, but a plain amateur video that depicts action and dialogue clearly is perfectly acceptable as a record of the show. I have programmed interstate shows on the strength of such DIY videos. Having said this, if you are serious about promoting your show for a touring circuit, it is in your best interests to fork out for a superior recording. You can then shoot the show from a couple of angles with sound recorded separately, and edit it properly. Some companies do special runs for the cameras, but a live shoot with a real audience is usually better. Whatever course you take, make sure that you record the *entire* show; an abridged version or highlights strung together will not convince potential presenters who want to get a sense of the whole production.

If you pitch a show to producers or funding bodies, don't expect *everyone* to watch the full video. Companies with touring experience often produce a three to five minute promotional video. This can be quite flashy, with fancy titles and music, scenes from the play, comments from the director and interviews with audience members as they leave the theatre. It's primarily a sales tool; if producers or venues like what they see, they can choose to watch the full version. You don't need a high level of video wizardry; a well-edited three to five minute segment with functional titles, that gives a *clear picture* of what the show is like (is it diverse in style; comic, dramatic, highly physical?) is a great start. Don't waste time being 'arty' at the expense of communicating the best things about your show—use your precious few minutes well. If you are using video footage for funding applications, this is particularly important, as committees often request to see support material during funding meetings. You have about one-and-a-half minutes to strut your stuff before someone calls 'enough', but they will keep going if it's great to watch. Make titles and fancy introductions very brief, or line up the video at the relevant point.

In addition to video material you will, of course, archive your great production photographs and all your marketing and advertising material. If you have hired a publicist they will provide press clippings in their final report; if not, you need to do so yourself. This can be time-consuming; hire a clipping service to do it if you want to keep a meticulous record of every listing. Together this forms the basis of great show documentation that can be quickly put together in different forms for any fabulous opportunities that arise. Do this for every show, and you may help to ensure the company's future. Even if the company doesn't stay together, the material will be of great use to its individual members.

Having paid no attention to archiving during the years when I co-ran an independent company in Sydney, I am eternally grateful to my partner in the venture, who meticulously clipped every article and review for eight years. When he presented the substantial folder to me, I had in my hands my history as an independent artist; an invaluable resource, which I have since used many times for job interviews and funding applications.

The life of the party

Is it possible to get more life out of your creation? Not every show needs (or deserves) another outing, but occasionally a small company will produce a work that is truly special, highly regarded by both audience and media, and perhaps a key point in its artistic development. A lot of companies think that mounting several shows in a year is the only way to build profile, but you can maintain presence (and possibly gain more artistically), by performing a great show that you are continuing to refine, to new audiences. Some commercial producers insist that their artists and companies develop a single work over a considerable period, so they can find resources concurrently for each stage, and then sell and tour it to a variety of locations, thus getting the most of a joint asset.

If you have performed a work in a season hub, it will be hard to get another season for it in the same city, unless it gets picked up by a substantially bigger venue or company. Ad-hoc productions, which may experience difficulty in getting everyone together again in six months time, should consider dovetailing the production with an interstate fringe festival or venue. These opportunities can be of great value for new and devised work, which may need more than one season to realise its full potential.

The experience of working in a foreign environment with few resources can be brutal, but it gives the company a chance to develop the show artistically, and much broader exposure, particularly if it is a festival hit (or wins awards). It's easier if company members already have contacts in the location. Before you make the decision to travel, it's wise to talk with other companies who've had the experience of being a 'foreign act' in that particular festival; you might decide that, if you can't get the venue or support you require, the effort of taking your show on the fringe festival road isn't worth it. But if you have a really strong show, and you think it would suit a season hub in another state, let the curator know it's on the boil, send an invitation in case they are in town, and pass on your fabulous documentation when it comes to hand. If you already have a history with them, or they know of your work, you may be able to set things up so that one season directly follows another, which can save you a lot of money with printing and promotional costs.

Touring

A much more substantial option may be to pitch your show to state (or interstate) touring networks. This takes company operations up a notch and is only suitable for companies with a dedicated core, including a well-organised and cluey producer and of course, a great show. The world of touring networks is very complex, involving long lead times and often multiple partners, including funding bodies. This area deserves a small book of its own, so I'll just discuss it briefly here, and direct you to some websites where you can start researching!

State and national touring networks

All states and territories have organisations who work with funding bodies to tour work (through presenter networks) into regional and outer-metropolitan areas: Arts on Tour in NSW and the ACT **[W46]**; Regional Arts Victoria in Victoria and Tasmania **[W47]**; Country Arts SA in South Australia **[W48]**; Country Arts WA in Western Australia **[W49]**; and the Queensland Arts Council in Queensland and the Northern Territory **[W50]**. Their websites contain detailed information about their processes for setting up tours within their own states and territories.

These bodies also form a unit called 'The Blue Heelers', who are the principal state touring coordinators and manage national touring. National touring is largely facilitated though two initiatives, 'Long Paddock' and 'CyberPaddock'. In the words of the Arts on Tour website:

> The Long Paddock is a forum that brings together venue managers, programmers, producers and touring agencies to discuss options for national touring in Australia and develop funding applications. CyberPaddock is a private web site initiated by the Blue Heelers that gives Australian presenters an opportunity to familiarise themselves with the available product prior to attending Long Paddock and to signal in advance those producers they would like to see make a presentation.

In short, producers can post information about their shows on CyberPaddock and those who attract the most interest from presenters (who log on separately and express interest in shows) are invited to pitch their project live at Long Paddock. As you can imagine, it's a very competitive field which attracts high-level submissions from small through to mainstream companies.

Performing Lines Australia **[W51]** is another unique organisation you should know about. In their own words:

> Performing Lines is funded by the Australia Council and Playing Australia to tour work, and only considers shows that have had fully produced seasons. They also produce for Major Arts Festivals and will auspice and produce creative developments for projects that have funding.

Performing Lines also manage tours for Mobile States, a national touring initiative for contemporary performance work. Mobile States links presenting partners Performance Space (Sydney), Brisbane

Powerhouse, Perth Institute of Contemporary Arts, Salamanca Arts Centre (Hobart) and Arts House—North Melbourne Town Hall. Details of programming policies can be found on the Performing Lines website.

Playing Australia **[W52]** (through the Australian Presenters Group) presents major tours by leading companies through professional performing arts centres, most of which are members of the Australasian Performing Arts Centres Association (APACA). It also provides grants for national touring to smaller companies, as well as producers, venues, presenters and tour organisers. They give priority to existing productions, and they like tours to include regional areas where possible. It's a federal funding program and highly competitive; there are two funding rounds each year which are widely advertised.

Do it yourself tours

Regional or outer-metropolitan touring in your own state is the first touring stepping stone for most small companies. It is possible to set up your own touring schedule and apply for touring costs through state and territory and federal funding bodies such as Playing Australia.

If you want to tour in your own state and you can get enough venues or presenters interested in the work, you can apply for net touring costs which include such things as accommodation, travel, freight and living allowances (state bodies won't usually fund remounting costs). In NSW, for example, the company could apply to the Performing Arts Touring Board of the NSW Ministry for the Arts **[W34],** which funds tours to, from and between regional centres. Companies are either funded directly or for Guarantee Against Loss (GAL). It's also worth checking out the website for Regional Arts NSW **[W53].** This is the peak body for the arts and community cultural development in regional and rural NSW and represents thirteen regional arts boards across the state. It is more relevant to regionally-based artists, but the development and program officers are very friendly and may be able to connect you with communities who are interested in hosting other work. Have a chat, too, with your local Blue Heeler organisations. Even if you don't get picked up through CyberPaddock or Long Paddock, the staff can help connect you with venues who may be interested in your work.

This may seem like a lot of hard work (it is!), but there are a number of government initiatives focused on developing regional artists, and in providing wider access to work that otherwise may only be seen in cities. It's been said to me many times that excellent small-scale work, such as that created by the professional independent community, is perfect for country touring. Not many companies consider it perhaps because they believe their work may be too risky for conservative regional audiences. But despite some tension, this is not always the case. Certainly, funding bodies (and local arts boards) are keen to bring innovative work to the regions. Do some research and talk to those in the know to find out if your show is suitable.

Finally, don't be disillusioned by rejection. Just because a show is turned down by one producer or programmer, doesn't mean it won't be just right for another festival, state or country. So fire up that computer and check out some of those websites!

Debriefing

Once the curtain comes down on the last show, you've bumped-out, celebrated wildly, reconciled monies and returned your very last prop, it's time to think about your final task—a debriefing session for the company. If it's been a 'fly-by-night' adventure, a drink at the pub will probably suffice, but if there's an enthusiastic company core, it's an invaluable growth exercise. The producer might also like to initiate a more formal meeting with the season hub curator, to dissect the production's artistic and producing strengths, but the company session is for your core stakeholders.

I suggest confining it to core members, the individuals who will continue to develop the company; but if you feel that any of the 'external' people involved, such as non-core actors or designers, might contribute effectively, include them as well. Create an agenda and a list of discussion points. If the production has been fraught with difficulty for whatever reason, this is a good time to talk, and hopefully defray tensions, but don't let it become a slanging match. The purpose of the session is to make things better for future productions. If it's likely a heated debate may ensue, then appoint a mediator (hopefully the producer), stick to the agenda and move on! Debrief discussion points may include:

- How does the company (honestly) rate the production artistically? What were its artistic strengths and weaknesses?
- One individual's show 'experience' may be very different from another's. Discuss company levels of support for each 'department'—how might they be improved?
- Discuss any 'systems' (financial, scheduling, communication paths etc). Did they operate effectively, or should things be done differently next time?
- What does the company think about providers and services that were used (graphic designers, printers, publicist etc), and their experience working in the chosen venue? What issues need to be addressed for future productions?
- Does the production have a life beyond this one?
- Did you gain enough professionally and enjoy the experience enough to do it all again?

Is the adventure over or is it just beginning? The extraordinary journey you've shared together will provide an answer to that question. Maybe it's been an arduous experience that's shown you the sheer hard work of getting an independent production on its feet; or perhaps you've had an exhilarating rollercoaster ride, and you feel that once is enough.

And maybe, if you've done it right, and luck has been with you, you will have achieved something more satisfying: lasting good company.

Web directory

[W1] **www.playworks.org.au**
Playworks

[W2] **www.ozscript.org**
The Australian Script Centre

[W3] **www.anpc.org.au**
Australian National Playwrights' Centre

[W4] **www.parnassusden.org.au**
Parnassus' Den

[W5] **www.nakedtheatrecompany.com.au**
Naked Theatre Company

[W6] **www.fairtrading.nsw.gov.au**
NSW Office of Fair Trading
Click on 'Business' for NSW and 'Related Sites' for other states

[W7] **www.business.gov.au**
Australian Government business gateway
Click on 'Thinking of Starting a Business'

[W8] **www.asic.gov.au/asic/asic.nsf**
Australian Securities and Investment Commission
Click on 'Search'

[W9] **www.alliance.org.au**
Media Entertainment and Arts Alliance

[W10] **Liquor licencing—state authorities:**
www.fairtrading.act.gov.au   ACT
Click on 'Business'
www.dgr.nsw.gov.au   NSW
www.nt.gov.au/ntt/licensing/liquor.shtml   NT
www.liquor.qld.gov.au   QLD
www.olgc.sa.gov.au   SA
www.treasury.tas.gov.au   TAS
www.consumer.vic.gov.au   VIC
Click on 'Business Licencing and Regulation'
www.orgl.wa.gov.au   WA

[W11] **www.copyright.org.au**
Australian Copyright Council

[W12] **www.artslaw.com.au**
Arts Law Centre of Australia

[W13] **www.apra.com.au**
Australian Performing Rights Association

[W14] **www.ppca.com.au**
Phonographic Performance Company

[W15] **www.showline.com.au**
The Association of Community Theatre

[W16] **www.duckforcover.com.au**
Duck for Cover

[W17] **www.ourcommunity.com.au**
Our Community
Click on 'Insurance and risk management centre'

[W18] www.niba.com.au
National Insurance Brokers Association

[W19] Workcover:
www.workcover.act.gov.au   ACT
www.workcover.nsw.gov.au   NSW
www.nt.gov.au/deet/worksafe   NT
www.workcover.qld.gov.au   QLD
www.workcover.com   SA
www.workcover.tas.gov.au   TAS
www.workcover.vic.gov.au   VIC
www.workcover.wa.gov.au   WA

[W20] www.microsoft.com
Microsoft Corporation
Click on 'Office' and then the 'Product'. Do a 'Template' search by typing in 'cash flow'.

[W21] www.artsatwork.com.au
Arts Up
Click on 'Arts Up'

[W22] www.abr.gov.au
Australian Business Register

[W23] www.ato.gov.au
Australian Tax Office

[W24] www.showcast.com.au
Showcast

[W25] www.artshub.com.au
Artshub Australia

[W26] www.theatre.asn.au
Theatre Australia

[W27] www.ozco.gov.au
Australia Council for the Arts

[W28] www.fuel4arts.com
fuel4arts

[W29] www.gettyimages.com
Getty Images

[W30] www.privacy.gov.au/publications/npps01.html
The Office of the Federal Privacy Commissioner

[W31] www.mediamonitors.com.au
Media Monitors

[W32] www.aap.com.au
AAP
Click on 'Products and Services'

[W33] www.mediaguide.com.au
Margaret Gee's Australian Media Guide

[W34] State funding bodies:
www.arts.act.gov.au   ACT
www.arts.nsw.gov.au   NSW
www.arts.nt.gov.au   NT
www.arts.qld.gov.au   QLD
www.arts.sa.gov.au   SA
www.arts.tas.gov.au   TAS
www.arts.vic.gov.au   VIC
www.dca.wa.gov.au/ArtsWA.asp   WA

[W35] www.artsinfo.net.au
Artsinfo

[W36] www.cultureandrecreation.gov.au
Culture and Recreation Portal

[W37] www.cultureandrecreation.gov.au/grants
Grants and Services Finder

[W38] www.theprogram.net.au
The Program

[W39] www.regionalarts.com.au
Regional Arts Australia

[W40] www.britishcouncil.org.au
British Council Australia

[W41] www.philanthropy.org.au
Philanthropy Australia

[W42] www.ianpotter.org.au
Ian Potter Foundation

[W43] www.ianpotter.org.au/ipct.html
Ian Potter Cultural Trust

[W44] www.abaf.org.au
Australian Business Arts Foundation

[W45] Gaming—state authorities:
www.gamblingandracing.act.gov.au   ACT
www.dgr.nsw.gov.au   NSW
www.nt.gov.au/ntt/licensing/gaming   NT
www.treasury.qld.gov.au/services/gambling/index   QLD
www.olgc.sa.gov.au   SA
www.treasury.tas.gov.au   TAS
www.vcgr.vic.gov.au   VIC
www.orgl.wa.gov.au   WA

[W46] www.artsontour.com.au
Arts on Tour

[W47] **www.rav.net.au**
Regional Arts Victoria

[W48] **www.countryarts.org.au**
Country Arts SA

[W49] **www.countryartswa.asn.au**
Country Arts WA

[W50] **www.qac.org.au**
Queensland Arts Council

[W51] **www.performinglines.org.au**
Performing Lines

[W52] **www.dcita.gov.au/arts/arts/playing_australia**
Playing Australia

[W53] **www.regionalartsnsw.com.au**
Regional Arts NSW

Index

THE POWER OF THE ACTOR
By Ivana Chubbuck
NOW AVAILABLE IN AUSTRALIA

Ivana Chubbuck is one of the most sought-after acting coaches and teachers in Hollywood. Her client list includes Brad Pitt, Charlize Theron, Elizabeth Shue, Jim Carrey, Kate Hudson, David Duchovny, and Halle Berry who famously thanked Chubbuck in her Oscar acceptance speech for *Monster's Ball*.

In THE POWER OF THE ACTOR the actor learns to truly find themselves within their character by endowing their situation and surroundings with emotional resonances drawn from their own experience. The book also shows the actor how to organically create sensations associated with certain commonly portrayed physical or emotional states such as substance abuse, sexual chemistry, fear, dying, pregnancy, parenthood, paralysis and emotional scars and bruises. From the acting coach with star power, this book will guide the actor to dynamic and effective results.

'Ivana Chubbuck is the premier acting coach of the twenty-first century. Under Ivana's tutelage, the course of my career and depth of my work have changed dramatically. Her book will be a saving grace to all aspiring actors and a gift to those of us who have been fortunate enough to practise this glorious craft.'
Halle Berry

'Ivana Chubbuck not only teaches us how to act fearlessly, but to live fearlessly.' Kate Bosworth

'Ivana Chubbuck's book will be a treasure for all students of acting, writing and directing.' Elisabeth Shue

ISBN 0 86819 779 3

THE COMEDY BIBLE
By Judy Carter

Are you funny? Want to have a career in comedy? This book can show you how to turn your sense of humour into a money-making career—and that's no joke!

Whether you yearn to create a killer stand-up act, write a sitcom, or be the star of your own one-person show, **Judy Carter** will help you develop your comedy skills and show you how to make money from being funny.

Written in Carter's unique, take-no-prisoners voice, THE COMEDY BIBLE is practical, inspirational and funny. Using a hands-on workbook format, this book offers a series of day-by-day exercises drawn from her wide experience as both a comic and comedy writer. Learn not only how to write jokes, speeches and scripts, but also where to sell them, how to pitch them, and even how to negotiate a contract. Along with providing additional 'insider' tips from her celebrity friends, Carter shows you ways you can turn comedy into cash that you have never thought of before.

'Until comedians can enrol in a comedy 101 humourversity course at the school of hard knock-knocks, this is the next best thing.'

Wil Anderson

ISBN 0 86819741 6

For a full list of our titles, visit our website:

www.currency.com.au

Currency Press
The performing arts publisher
PO Box 2287
Strawberry Hills NSW 2012
Australia
enquiries@currency.com.au
Tel: (02) 9319 5877
Fax: (02) 9319 3649